A Catamount Christmas

Catamount Lion Shifters

By J. H. Croix

This is a work of fiction. Names, characters, businesses, places, events and incidents are either the products of the author's imagination or used in a fictitious manner. Any resemblance to actual persons, living or dead, or actual events is purely coincidental.

ISBN: 1537727745
ISBN 13: 9781537727745

Dedication

Cheers to holiday romance!

Sign up for my newsletter for information on new releases!

http://jhcroix.com/page4/

Follow me!

jhcroix@jhcroix.com
https://twitter.com/JHCroix
https://www.facebook.com/jhcroix

Chapter 1

Roxanne Morgan spun around and passed a sandwich over the counter, immediately turning to take the order of the next person in line. She was covering the deli counter for lunch at the small business she owned—a grocery store, hardware store and deli all rolled into one.

"What'll it be?" she asked, her eyes quickly scanning the area beyond the counter. When there was no reply, she glanced up. Her heart stuttered and then lunged forward into a wild pounding.

"Hey Roxy," the man standing across the counter said.

Roxanne didn't find herself speechless very often, but at the moment, she couldn't seem to form a word. Max Stone stood in front of her—the one and only boy she'd ever loved, the boy who'd broken her heart when he left Catamount, Maine…and their love behind. Her eyes soaked him in—his mahogany brown hair, his amber eyes, and his lanky, muscled body. He wore a black down jacket,

1

unzipped to reveal a charcoal gray shirt and faded jeans. His gaze coasted over her. She felt bare and exposed, and frantically tried to gather herself together inside.

Her cheeks felt hot, but she ignored it. She could do this. All she had to do was be polite. Her body was only reacting because she hadn't seen Max in so long. It was an echo of their past and nothing more. "Hey Max. Haven't seen you around in years," she finally replied, her words belying the turmoil she felt inside.

The truth was it had been precisely fifteen years since Max had been in Catamount. He had moved away with his mother after his father died in an accident at the mill in a nearby town. Roxanne and Max had started dating the year before, and she'd loved him in the way only youth allowed—head over heels infatuation mingled with the rosy yearning to be together forever. The hopes of youth had kept her tendency toward cynicism at bay, and she'd flung herself into their relationship. One afternoon when Max was supposed to come over, he'd called instead. In a conversation that lasted maybe five minutes, he told her his father had died, they were moving, and he broke up with her. She'd been too stunned to fully absorb what he said. A few days later when she managed to cobble together a coherent thought, she'd raced over to his house to try to talk to him and found his family's home locked up. No one answered the door after she knocked for what felt like hours.

She'd swung between the emotional poles of grief, about his father and about the abrupt end of their relationship. She'd stuffed her grief away and done her damnedest to move on. The first few years after he left, she would occasionally wonder if she might hear from him, or if he would return to Catamount. She finally gave up hoping and wishing, but she never quite got over Max.

Now, he stood here before her and a tornado of feelings swirled through her—confusion, hope, joy, anger, sadness and more. She twirled a pen between her fingers and wondered what to do. A small part of her wanted to storm past him and not look back, just the way he'd left her all those years ago. She couldn't do that though because she owned Roxanne's Country Store. An arc of annoyance flashed through her. Max was showing up in the heart of her world.

"It's really good to see you, Roxy," Max said, cutting through her short walk down memory lane.

Max happened to be the only person who'd ever called her Roxy with any regularity. It chafed to hear him call her that now.

She willed herself to stay calm. Still struggling to form words sensibly, she nodded. She couldn't quite bring herself to say it was good to see him. She was relieved when another customer stepped to the counter.

Hank Anderson, Catamount's police chief, leaned against the counter. "Hey Roxanne, can I get the usual today?"

Roxanne glanced to Hank. "Sure. Give me a sec." She forced a smile and turned away to pour a cup of coffee for Hank. At the moment, she would have given just about anything to have Becky here to help this morning. Becky was one of her regular deli employees and would normally be here, but she'd called in sick with a nasty cold. Roxanne was reconsidering how relieved she'd been to not be exposed to whatever the hell Becky had. She sounded like she was on the verge of death when she called, so Roxanne had happily supported her staying home until she was better. But now, with Max here, Roxanne didn't have any back up, so she couldn't busy herself in the back of the kitchen. She had no choice but to stay here and somehow

3

fumble through the next few minutes. She prayed Max wouldn't stay long. As she fitted the lid over Hank's coffee, she heard him start talking to Max and anxiety tightened in her chest.

"Max Stone? Damn, haven't seen you around in years! How are ya?" Hank asked.

Roxanne turned back to face them, gripping Hank's coffee tightly in her hand. Max grinned over at Hank. "Hey Hank, it's good to see you. It might have been a long time, but I'm back to stay."

Roxanne felt as if she were falling inside. Max was back to stay? So many questions tumbled through her mind, she couldn't think clearly. She mentally shook herself. It had been fifteen years. She was long past her youthful love for him, and he'd clearly never felt the same way. If he had, she didn't see how he could have left things between them the way he did and then just walk in here casually. Anger rose inside, but she batted it back. She needed to stay calm and not make a scene.

Max and Hank were still talking when she turned and took the few steps to the counter. She set Hank's coffee down and slid it over. "Here you go"

Hank snagged it and took a gulp. "Ahh. Perfect." He pulled his wallet out, glancing between Roxanne and Max as he did. "Did you two stay in touch all these years?" Hank asked.

His question was innocent enough, but it sent another flash of anger through Roxanne. She wasn't up for nosy questions. She busied herself taking the ten-dollar bill Hank handed over and getting his change from the register, her ears perked to see how Max responded to Hank's question.

"Unfortunately not," Max replied. "Things were a little hectic that first year after my dad died, and I wasn't thinking too clearly."

Roxanne couldn't stop herself from looking over to Max. His amber eyes caught hers. "Roxanne was the first person I looked for when I got here, so I'm hoping we'll have time to catch up."

Hank chuckled. "Roxanne's Country Store here is still the heart and soul of Catamount. She's done her family proud running it the way she does." Hank took another swallow of coffee. "Anyway, good to see you, Max. If you need anything, just stop by. Where you staying?"

"My mom never sold our old house, so I'm planning to renovate it. Until then, I booked a room at the inn down the street."

Hank pushed away from the counter. "Well, you've got your work cut out for you. Don't think anybody's been there since you left."

Something flashed in Max's eyes. Once upon a time, Roxanne might have thought it was pain, but she wouldn't know right now. Though her body was spinning with heat and the familiarity of Max's presence, her mind was bolting steel doors around her heart and insisting she not go thinking she knew him the way she once did.

"I'm sure I do. I plan to head up there in a little bit to take a look. Good to see you, Hank."

"If you need any help, let me know. I'm sure I can round up a few kids from the high school to help out with the land clearing. They're young and too strong to worry about their backs yet," Hank said as he lifted his coffee cup in a farewell and turned away.

Max turned back to the counter. For a long moment, he didn't say anything. He simply looked at her, his eyes coasting over her face and dipping down before returning. Her cheeks heated when his gaze met hers again. "I'm guessing this feels kind of out of the blue for you, huh?"

Her heart in her throat, Roxanne nodded.

Max curled his hands on the edge of the counter. "I have enough sense to know now probably isn't a great time to talk, but I just need you to know I'm sorry. I couldn't have stopped my mom from up and leaving Catamount the way we did right after my dad died, but I shouldn't have broken things off with you the way I did."

Another customer approached the counter. Gail Anderson, Hank's wife, stepped to Max's side. "I just saw Hank on his way out," Gail said, not even bothering with a perfunctory greeting.

With her mind spinning over what Max had just said, Roxanne turned to Gail, barely able to think. She must have managed to nod because Gail huffed. "I told him I was only running a few minutes behind!" Gail's blue eyes snapped. Gail and Hank were long-time Catamount residents, both born and raised here, and entwined in the community. Hank was the police chief and Gail was a retired schoolteacher. Gail glanced to her side, her eyes widening. "Max Stone?"

Oh. My. God. Just how many of these moments am I going to have to survive? Well, Max's family was here for a long time before they left. Anyone that knew him is going to be startled to see him. You'd better get used to this. Roxanne mentally sighed as she tried to marshal her thoughts. *It might mean nothing that Max said he shouldn't have broken things off the way he did. He might not have felt the way you did anyway, he just feels bad about how he handled it. Don't go thinking it's anything other than that. Just act normal and get through this.*

Roxanne cued in to the conversation between Max and Gail. "I decided to move back last summer after my mom died. Her sister was the reason we moved there, and she died the year before, so there was nothing left holding me there. I missed Catamount the entire time we were gone, so I decided it was time to come home," Max said.

Gail looked between Max and Roxanne, her eyes considering. She appeared about to say something, but she stayed quiet for several beats. "Well, it's nice to have you back. I missed your mother. I'm sorry to hear she passed away."

Max nodded solemnly. "I wish she'd had a chance to get back here before she died."

Gail nodded firmly. "It is what it is. Everyone will be glad to know you're here." She turned to Roxanne. "I was supposed to meet Hank for coffee, but since he couldn't be bothered to wait, I'll get some to go."

Roxanne felt like she was in a surreal dream. On autopilot, she swung around and poured a cup of coffee for Gail. Moments later, Gail was walking through the deli and down one of the grocery aisles to the front door.

When Roxanne turned back to Max, she forced herself to keep it light because she couldn't deal with anything else right now. "What can I get for you?" she asked, her words coming out smoothly only because she'd said them thousands of times.

***

Max looked over at Roxanne and tamped down the urge to leap over the counter and pull her into his arms. She stood there before him, her blonde hair pulled back in a haphazard ponytail, loose curls escaping and framing her heart-shaped face. Her blue eyes were as gorgeous as he remembered—wide eyes that tipped up at the corners, the blue so rich he could lose himself in it. Not a day had passed since he left when he didn't think about her, and here she stood before him—taking his breath away. Fifteen years later, she'd filled out and her figure was all curves—

7

generous breasts, an hourglass dip at her waist, and lush hips. She emanated a strength and power she hadn't had back when they were young. She'd always been strong and independent, so it didn't surprise him to sense those qualities had blossomed within her.

Max had so much to say, yet now clearly was not the time or place. Roxanne's Country Store was bustling. The deli area where they were now had customers seated at tables scattered throughout the small area. The rest of the store, a mix of groceries, hardware and just about everything, had customers meandering through the aisles as they filled shopping baskets. This place held so many memories for him, it was almost overwhelming.

Fifteen years ago, he came home from school to find his mother had already packed up everything in his bedroom and announced they were moving to Virginia. That morning, his father had died in an accident at the paper mill in a neighboring town. The police had shown up at school to tell him and driven him home. His mother's eyes had been puffy and red, and the only thing that seemed to hold her together was the drive to get out of Catamount as quickly as possible. Max was emotionally reeling and didn't know what to think about anything. He still didn't know why he'd broken up with Roxanne when he called her to tell her what happened. He'd replayed that conversation in his mind over and over again. The only conclusion he could come to was he'd been in such shock between his father's death and his mother's abrupt announcement that he thought everything was ending at once.

He'd stumbled through the next few weeks, twisted and turned in the emotional turmoil of his father's death, his mother's grief and trying to adjust to living somewhere new. He'd been born and raised in Catamount, Maine—a shifter stronghold and the founding community of all shifters. Being born into a family of shifters, when they moved to Virginia, he'd been forced to adjust to a life of secrecy. Until the year before his mother died, he'd never quite understood why they left Catamount. The years passed and he never forgot Roxanne. Every so often, he thought about calling her. Once, he actually did. Her mother had answered and told him in no uncertain terms that he'd broken Roxanne's heart, which devastated him. Whether or not she told Roxanne he called, he didn't know. After that, he'd never gathered the nerve to call Roxanne again.

He looked over at Roxanne. A sharp pain slashed through him to see the guarded expression in her eyes. He wanted to make things right with her. Now. He started to say something when yet another customer approached the counter. Blessedly, whoever this was didn't seem to know him. They ordered a sandwich and went to sit at one of the small round tables. Roxanne caught his eyes. "If you'd like to order, now would be the time."

There was a sharp edge to her voice, which cut him to the core. He *needed* to fix this with her. Max fought back the urge to ask her if they could talk now. "Right. I can see you're busy. I'll take a coffee."

She spun away and stepped behind another counter to make the requested sandwich. She called out when it was ready, handing it over to the customer, before she got his coffee ready. When she slid the bright blue paper coffee cup across the counter, his heart gave a hard kick. He remembered spending many afternoons here with her. She was still using the same cups her parents used when they ran the store. She was busy doing something at the register. He waited, hoping she would pause. When she didn't, he moved to stand in front of the register. This was too important, so he wasn't walking away just yet.

"Roxy?"

Her eyes whipped up. For a flash, he saw pain and something else there, but she quickly shuttered it. He forged ahead. "Look, I'm hoping we can talk. Soon. I missed you. More than I can even say. I'll go now because I know you're working, but maybe I could take you out for dinner or something?"

Roxanne stared at him for so long, uncertainty began to slide through him. He heard her take a deep breath and close her eyes. When she opened them, she looked right at him. "Okay. Fine. We might as well get this over with. Tonight's no good because Becky's out sick, so I'll be here until closing. How about tomorrow?"

He couldn't keep from smiling. "Tomorrow's perfect. Six o'clock work?"

She nodded slowly. He reached over and grabbed a small pad of paper and a pen sitting by the register. He quickly jotted down his cell number. "Just so you have it."

**

Roxanne watched Max leave. He wove through the tables and headed down the center aisle, his lean body ambling, yet giving off a sense of leashed power. His dark hair glinted in the sun cast through the front windows. He looked back when he reached the door, and she felt as if there was an invisible current between them. Even from across the room with tables and aisles between them, she felt that shimmering connection. She forced her eyes away and looked up at the next customer, wondering if she'd gone and lost her mind by so quickly agreeing to have dinner with him.

Chapter 2

When Max got outside, he looked both directions on Main Street before his eyes landed on the sign to the store—Roxanne's Country Store, We Have Everything. His heart swelled. Once he'd gotten the nerve to ask Roxanne out all those years ago in high school, he stopped by this store after school almost every day to see her. He had nothing but good memories tied to this place. His eyes moved on, taking in the picturesque town green and the tidy tree-lined streets. Catamount was a fairly typical New England town in Maine. Its most distinctive detail was a well-guarded secret—the existence of mountain lion shifters. Max hadn't realized how hard it would be to hide the duality of who he was until he lived away from Catamount. This morning when he'd seen the highway exit to Catamount, his entire being had relaxed a little. It wasn't that shifters ran around shifting in the open in Catamount, but at least here he knew he was surrounded by other shifters who understood who and what he was.

He stood on the sidewalk probably too long, mostly because he had to rein in the urge to turn around and walk back into the store to see Roxy again. She was everything he remembered and more. He had to wait a full day and then some to get his chance to talk to her. Given that he'd waited fifteen years, he figured he could handle it. He hadn't counted on how strong his pull to her would be the moment he laid eyes on her. The lion inside knew with unshakable certainty that she was meant to be his. He had to find a way to convince her guarded heart of that truth. He could only hope she'd forgive him for leaving all those years ago.

He took a gulp of the delicious coffee she'd made him and finally began to walk to his car, a black SUV parked across the street. He climbed inside and steeled himself to go to his childhood home. The home was only minutes from downtown Catamount, along a winding mountain road.

Catamount had started centuries ago as a small town deep in the woods of Maine, tucked in the foothills of the Appalachian Mountains. At the time, mountain lions were struggling to survive as a species as their territory shrunk year after year with humans expanding into their lands. As such, they were considered largely extinct in the East and had been for over seventy-five years. What was missing from that account was the fact that a few centuries back, high in the Appalachian Mountains on the famed Mount Katahdin, a litter of mountain lions was born with the inexplicable ability to shift from lion to human and back. This genetic quirk carried on among a strain of mountain lions with the purely wild Eastern mountain lions dying out, while their shifter counterparts survived against all odds.

Catamount was south of Mount Katahdin in the

Appalachian Range where the mountains were smaller and where lakes were plentiful. The once small town had grown over the centuries to a mid-size bustling community. Shifters lived amidst humans, their existence a well-guarded secret. Max's mind spun back to the afternoon he arrived home from school after learning his father had died. In the span of a few short hours, his life was turned upside down, and he was taken far away from the sanctuary of Catamount. He shook his head sharply as he rounded a curve in the road. He didn't need to dwell. He was back here now and the one and only woman who held his heart was here. He just had to find a way to reclaim her.

Max rounded another bend in the road and slowed in front of the driveway to his family's home. He recalled Hank's comment that the property was overgrown. That might have been a mild understatement. Vines had taken hold in the trees in the front of the property, almost completely shielding the home from view. He turned into the driveway, which was overgrown with weeds and grass, and rolled slowly around the semi-circle driveway before coming to a stop. The home was a classic cape style and had once been charming. The same couldn't be said now. Weeds abounded in his mother's old flowerbeds. Several shutters hung loose while a few had fallen to the ground. The home was in dire need of a fresh coat of paint, and it appeared several windows also needed to be replaced.

He slowly climbed out of his car, memories assailing him. He approached the home and climbed up the steps. He fished his old house key out of his pocket. In another moment, he was standing inside the dusty home. He couldn't help but wonder if anyone had entered this home since the day he and his mother left. He hadn't thought to ask her if she'd had anyone check on the home all these years. A cursory walk around revealed someone must've stopped by, likely in the early days after they left, to empty and clean the refrigerator. It was dusty, but otherwise clean. The cabinets in the kitchen were also empty. He slowly circled the downstairs, which was a typical cape layout with a living room and dining room separated by the stairs. The kitchen and a bathroom with laundry were to the back of the downstairs.

He climbed the stairs, which led to a short hallway that held three bedrooms. A bath was off the hallway, along with another in the master bedroom. He peeked into his parents' old bedroom first to find the furniture there, but everything else emptied out. With a breath, he turned and walked past the empty guestroom to his old bedroom. Just as with the other rooms, it was bare save for the furniture. His stomach felt hollow. He stepped to the window that looked out over the yard. A tumbledown stone wall circled the large yard. The home was tucked in a dip between two hills, not quite a valley because Catamount was in the foothills of the mountains. A small stream wound along the hillside and crossed the back corner of the yard with two small arches in the stone wall accommodating it.

As he scanned the view, memories of afternoons spent with Roxanne slammed into him. Back then, he'd looked for any and every chance to find time alone with her, so he'd thrown himself into making his old tree house nice enough to bring Roxanne there. His father had gamely helped him drag beanbag chairs up the rickety ladder. They'd gone on to spend many an afternoon lounging in them when the weather was nice. Only a few boards remained in the tree, the rest clustered on the ground, likely blown down by wind over the years.

He recalled leaving in a rush and that his mother had packed most of his belongings before he arrived home. All those years of wondering why they left so abruptly sent a flash of anger through him. He might have more of an answer now than he ever did, but it hurt. Seeing Roxy made him wish he'd been a little older and wiser at the time. He'd missed her with every fiber of his being for so long, missing her had woven itself into his life. Looking back, he wished he could've found a way to handle everything differently. Between reeling from his father's death and his mother's insistence that he had to cut ties with anyone in Catamount, he hadn't known what else to do other than say goodbye. He only hoped he could have the second chance he wanted with Roxy.

He turned away from the window, shuttering his memories, and jogged back downstairs. He needed to get back to town and get checked into the inn until he could get the house in shape.

***

Roxanne rolled the full rack of dishes into the industrial dishwasher in the back of the deli kitchen. Once the rack clicked into place, she tapped the button to start the machine and stepped to the sink to wash her hands. The deli closed a full hour earlier than the rest of the store, which Roxanne appreciated because it gave her time to clean up and make sure the schedule was set for the following day. The store had been running smoothly for decades by the time she formally took over after her father passed away. Her mother had a stroke the year before her father died, so for all intents and purposes, Roxanne had been managing the store long before it was officially hers.

She'd savored the busy work throughout the day as she tried to stop obsessing over Max Stone's abrupt reappearance in Catamount. From what he'd said, it sounded as if he planned to stay. Until she'd seen him today, she'd convinced herself that her memories of how powerful their connection had been were overblown. Then, he'd walked into her life again. In a flash, his very presence wiped out her confidence that she'd moved on and obliterated any idea that she'd imagined the depth of their connection. It was like a living, breathing force connected them. She didn't like how much power he held over her heart.

She pulled off her apron and tossed it in the laundry hamper in the back corner before making her way to the front of the store. Diane Franklin finished ringing up a customer and leaned her hip on the register counter when she saw Roxanne approaching.

"You heading upstairs for the night?" Diane asked with a grin as the customer exited the store.

"Just checking to see if we have tomorrow's shifts covered up front."

Diane turned and clicked the screen to the scheduler. Her long dark hair, streaked with silver, hung in a braid down her back, which swung as she turned back to face Roxanne. "All set. Need any extra help in the deli? You were working double all day with Becky out." Diane managed the front end of the store. She'd started working for Roxanne's parents years ago. Roxanne didn't know what she'd have done without Diane's steady hand. It gave Roxanne room to do what she enjoyed most—the cooking and bantering that came with the deli—and time to handle the behind the scenes work of ordering, accounting and then some for the store and deli.

Roxanne leaned against the opposite side of the counter from Diane and shrugged. "I'll manage. Tomorrow's not her regular shift anyway."

Diane's brown eyes coasted over Roxanne. "Okay. If you need help after that, I could find someone to cover."

Roxanne shook her head. "Don't call anyone. It's

just a few days. Anyway, how'd things go up here today?"

"Same, same. Always busy." Diane paused, her eyes considering. "So, Max Stone is back in town?"

Roxanne's stomach flipped at the sound of his name, while her heart clenched and emotions swirled inside —anger and pain offset by an intense longing. His appearance had set off a tornado inside of her. Any spare moment when she wasn't completely preoccupied today, she'd wondered what it meant when he said he missed her. She desperately wanted to know if he'd missed her the way she missed him. Countering that desperation was her anger with herself for caring so damn much about him. She finally met Diane's eyes. "Guess so." Her brief comment belied the turmoil she felt inside.

Diane nodded slowly. "How do you feel about that? I mean, you and him, well, everyone thought you'd be together forever."

Roxanne wanted to cry at Diane's comment. She'd thought they'd be together forever too, and it stung like hell to have that dream ripped away. At that moment, the bell over the door jingled and Shana Thorne walked in. Shana's dark blonde hair blew in a swirl with the soft gust of wind that followed her through the door. Closing the door behind her, she smoothed her hair and glanced over to the check out counter. "Hey, didn't expect to see you up here," she said, her blue-gray eyes crinkling at the corners with her smile when she saw Roxanne.

Roxanne shrugged. "I'm all finished up out back."

Shana's eyes shifted to Diane. "I forgot I was out of flour after I already started baking."

Diane grinned. "Good thing we're open 'til ten. Hang on, I'll grab your flour." Diane rounded the corner of the counter and headed down one of the aisles.

Shana reached Roxanne's side and leaned against

the counter beside her. "How's it going?"

Roxanne shrugged again. "Okay." Shana was one of her closest friends, so Roxanne was wrestling with the pull to tell her about Max when Diane returned, holding a bag of flour aloft.

"Here you go," Diane said, setting the flour on the counter and quickly ringing Shana up.

Shana paid, her eyes flicking back to Roxanne as she returned her wallet to her purse. "So what's up?" she asked generally.

Roxanne swallowed against the emotion welling inside. Shana had been there for her after Max left. At seventeen years old, she'd been young and hurting in the way only angsty teenagers can hurt. Shana and a few of Roxanne's closest friends had circled the wagons and helped her get through his abrupt breakup and move away. Roxanne didn't know if she wanted to relive the turbulence only Max seemed to elicit inside of her.

Diane piped up. "Max Stone is back in town. He stopped by today. Rumor has it he's here to stay."

Shana's eyes widened and swung to Roxanne. "Oh. Wow. Did he talk to you?"

Roxanne nodded and sighed. "Yeah. He came to the deli and got a coffee."

"And?" Shana asked, circling her hand.

"And said he missed me and we needed to talk."

Two pairs of eyes widened as her friends looked at her. She almost laughed.

"He actually said that?" Shana asked.

Roxanne nodded emphatically. "Uh huh. No idea what to think. Hank happened to be here when Max was here. He told Hank he planned to stay. I guess his mother never sold their old house." She was simply stating a few details, but the concrete reality of Max being here was starting to sink in and it made her feel panicky inside.

Shana eyed her for a long moment and angled her head to the side. "Sooo…how do you feel about all this?"

Diane glanced to Shana. "I asked her the same thing right before you showed up."

Roxanne was accustomed to being more in control of her feelings and was usually the one who could throw out a sarcastic comment to lighten the mood. Right now, she couldn't seem to find any of her jaunty humor to pull her through. She felt like she'd been thrown back to those first few months after Max left and she had to face her first heartbreak. Well, her only heartbreak because she'd never let anyone get as close to her again. She took a deep breath, trying to ease the tension in her chest. She looked over at her two friends—Shana who'd shared every phase of her life with her growing up in Catamount, and Diane who was more like an overprotective aunt and the closest link to her parents since they both passed away.

"I have no idea how to feel about any of it. I have a ton of questions for him, and I'm still kinda pissed off. I guess I thought I wasn't, but then I haven't seen him in fifteen years, so there's that."

Shana stepped closed and slipped an arm over her shoulders. "Well, that makes sense. If you need any of us to kick his ass, just say so."

That brought a wry smile. Roxanne glanced over to Shana. "Good to know. I guess I'll finally get the chance I wanted to find out what the hell happened."

Chapter 3

The following morning, Max stood in the center of his hotel room and glanced around. Funny how he finally managed to find his way back home, and yet he still felt like he was living a borrowed life. It wasn't that he'd expected his family's home to be in great shape, he just hadn't been prepared for how empty and barren it felt there. Fifteen years and all he'd ever wanted was to get back to Catamount where he felt like he was home. Having seen Roxy finally, he wasn't sure if his longing to return to Catamount was because of the place or because of her. He'd rented a room at Catamount Inn. A massive old mansion, built over two hundred years ago, had been renovated into a lovely bed and breakfast to cater to the tourists that flocked to Catamount and many other towns in Maine throughout the summer and winter. Maine had the blessing of warm summers with the ocean on one side of the state and the mountains on the other. Winter brought the skiers for visits. While Catamount didn't have its own ski lodge, a neighboring town did, so Catamount reaped the benefits.

Max's suite consisted of a lovely old bedroom with a sitting room to one side and a bathroom with a massive claw foot tub. The owners kept the home true to its era with gleaming oak flooring, high ceilings and tall windows throughout the inn. The inn was furnished with antiques in the simple Shaker style favored in this area. While they kept the inn aesthetically historical, they added modern amenities as well. The old radiators were purely decorative now and the bathroom had been entirely updated.

He'd sold his mother's home in Virginia and just about everything in it before he came back to Catamount. He'd been determined to close that chapter of his life, so he had. As such, all he had with him was the duffel he'd tossed on the floor by the dresser and a few boxes wending their way to him through the mail. He turned to the window facing Main Street and pushed the curtain back. Roxanne's Country Store was visible down the street. The store was housed in another lovely old home. All of New England was dotted with these original homes, many lovingly maintained over centuries. The store was in a stately colonial home on a corner. Roxanne's grandfather had started the store during the Great Depression and renamed it after her when she was born. He'd moved his young family into the two upper floors of the three-story home and renovated the entire first floor into a store. The store had gone on to become such a fixture in Catamount, Max couldn't imagine the community without it.

He wondered how Roxanne had been all these years. He'd done a little online sleuthing before he came back, mostly because he didn't dare cling to the hope he might have a chance with her if she was committed otherwise. He knew she wasn't married, but he didn't know much else. It didn't surprise him, but Roxanne wasn't too active online. He turned away from the window, letting the curtain fall. He snagged his jacket off the hook by the door.

Moments later, he was walking down the street with no particular destination in mind. He had to physically force himself to turn in the direction away from Roxanne's store. If his lion side could dictate what he did, he'd march straight to her again. He reminded himself, quite sternly, that he'd be seeing her tonight. He could've used a cup of her coffee, but he'd find something else. There were many familiar stores lining the streets of Catamount, but a few newer ones as well. He pushed through the swinging door of a gas station where he helped himself to the coffee and a muffin from the tiny deli there before retracing his steps to the inn.

He ate at a small table by the windows, staring out over the town. Catamount was in the midst of harvest season with Thanksgiving and Christmas not far off. Town workers were hanging holiday lights along the streets. Max's chest felt funny when he realized he had no family here to celebrate the holidays with. Growing up, his family had been woven deeply into the community. The shifter community was tight-knit and his parents had both been born and raised in Catamount. His grandparents had passed away before his father died, which left no one behind from their family in Catamount. Over the years, his family often joined a number of other shifter families for holiday gatherings at Roxanne's Country Store. He wondered if that tradition had carried on, and more specifically, if he'd manage to repair his relationship with Roxy enough to be able to join in. Even though he'd spent years tolerating the echoing loss of Roxy in his life, he hadn't been prepared for how it would affect him to see her. The constant beat of missing her had morphed into an intense, visceral longing for her now that she was within his reach.

***

Roxanne moved quickly, emptying the boxes of deli supplies that had arrived with this morning's delivery. Normally, she assigned the storeroom stocking to Joey Anderson, Gail and Hank's nephew. At seventeen years old, he was young, strong and a hard worker. He did a little bit of everything around the store. She'd tried to get through the usual inventory data entry, but she was so distracted by thoughts of Max, she couldn't focus. She hefted a box containing various condiments on the counter and began pulling them out and stocking the shelves. She couldn't turn her brain off, but at least it didn't matter if she wasn't thinking straight with this task.

Max's words kept playing on repeat in her mind. *"I missed you. More than I can even say."* Those two sentences rang like a bell inside of her, stirring up old hopes and dreams she'd long ago let drift away. She shook her head sharply and quickly placed the last item on the shelf, broke down the empty box, tossed it roughly in the corner of the room and grabbed the next box.

"Geez, are you mad at the blue cheese dressing, or something?"

Roxanne glanced over her shoulder to find Phoebe North standing in the doorway of the storeroom. Like Shana, Phoebe was an old childhood friend. Her dark eyes held a gleam of mischief. Roxanne slowed her motion and set the bottle of dressing on the shelf and gave it a little push. She had practically been throwing the bottles on the shelf. She turned to lean against the table nearby and shrugged.

"So what if I'm mad at the blue cheese dressing?" she asked.

Phoebe stepped into the room and leaned her hip against the table. "I'm guessing you're not," she countered with a short laugh. She brushed her dark hair off her shoulders. "Don't you usually have Joey handle the stocking?"

Roxanne nodded. "Usually. Just felt like doing it myself today."

Phoebe eyed her, and Roxanne suddenly felt like she was under a microscope. The downside to having friends who'd known you forever was they noticed just about everything. Roxanne also figured word of Max's return had traveled through Catamount by now.

Phoebe didn't waste time getting right to the point. "I heard Max Stone is back in town and he happened to be here yesterday."

Roxanne nodded, her stomach churning and her chest tightening. She hated how quickly Max's sudden reappearance in her life had turned her inside and out, and shown her just how much she hadn't gotten past him. It was so much easier to believe she'd long ago moved on from him when she didn't have to face him. She couldn't help but wonder if she was seriously insane to have agreed to dinner with him. Yet, she couldn't find it in her to back out now. Every time she thought about it, her heart pleaded with her not to shut him out.

Phoebe's gaze shifted from curious to concerned. "Are you okay?"

Roxanne shrugged. "I'm fine. It's just... I don't know...out of the blue. He's here and apparently he plans to stay. He said he missed me and wanted to talk and now I feel all crazy inside. I thought..." Her words trailed off because she didn't know how to explain her muddled feelings.

Phoebe, who'd been there day in and day out after

Max left town, took two steps and enveloped Roxanne in a hug. When she stepped back, she ran her hands down Roxanne's arms and gave a little squeeze. "You loved him so much. It was always going to be weird if he showed up again."

Roxanne swallowed against the tightness in her throat and nodded. "Yeah, it's weird. I guess I thought he'd never come back, so I didn't think about what it might be like if he did. I wish I knew what he wanted."

"He said he missed you? How long was he here?"

"Oh, maybe five minutes. He came to the deli yesterday afternoon. He said he wanted to talk and asked me to dinner. Like an idiot, I said yes." Roxanne flinched internally at the tinge of bitterness in her words. Her young, teenaged self was still in her heart, still hurt and angry at how things had played out between them, while her older, wiser self liked to think she'd moved past it all. That tinge of bitterness hinted perhaps she hadn't.

Phoebe's dark gaze was thoughtful. "Maybe it's best just to clear the air. If he does anything to hurt you again, we'll run him out of town this time."

A little laugh bubbled up. "Right." Roxanne's smile faded. "It probably is best to clear the air, but hell, this is so out of nowhere. I hate how it makes me feel."

"Yeah, well, he's here, so you're kinda stuck with that." Phoebe paused, watching Roxanne for a few beats. "What are you gonna do if he wants to try again? I mean, he said he missed you. Since he said that within the first few minutes of seeing you, I'm guessing he wasn't just being nice."

Hope sparked inside, a hot flame she couldn't seem to extinguish. Annoyance with herself and at her apparent weakness flared behind the hope. Max was the only man who had this effect on her, but she chalked it up to youth before. They'd been seventeen and head over heels in love and lust the way only youth allowed. She didn't know if the wild mess of feelings inside now was simply the echo of what once was, or the banked embers of something that never died.

Roxanne met Phoebe's concerned gaze and shrugged. "I have no idea. I never thought I'd see him again. I hate how mixed up inside I am. All he did was show up and I'm all a mess!"

"You're not a mess, you're just used to always being on control. Maybe it will be weird, but I say have dinner with him and say your piece. If he's here to stay, either you spend all kinds of time avoiding him, or just get through this. Maybe it won't be anything, maybe it will. Except for how things ended with you two, Max was always a good guy. Maybe you can finally find out what the hell happened. When are you supposed to meet him for dinner?"

"Tonight."

"Geez, he's not wasting any time is he?"

Another laugh bubbled up. Phoebe's wry humor helped ease the churning tightness inside. "Guess not."

"Hey Roxanne, did we get any boxes of flour for out front?" Diane's question preceded her as she strode down the hall and poked her head around the corner of the storeroom. "Oh hey!" she said with a grin when she saw Phoebe.

"I haven't gotten to that part of the shipment yet. Give me a few minutes, okay?" Roxanne asked.

Diane nodded. "Got it. I thought we had more, but one of the teachers from the elementary school came by this morning and cleaned us out for some baking science project." The doorbell chimed out front, and she spun away. "Let me know if we have any," she called over her shoulder.

"I'll get going. Call me if you need to tonight," Phoebe said before stepping to Roxanne and giving her another quick hug.

After Phoebe disappeared through the doorway, Roxanne remained still for a moment, staring at the shelves. She needed to just get through this day and somehow get through dinner. She couldn't help but hope a little more time with Max would show her that her feelings yesterday had been nothing more than a reaction to the surprise of seeing him again. She was over him…she had to be.

Chapter 4

Max stood on the sidewalk beside the town green, his eyes idly following the granite walkways crisscrossing the green. He lifted his gaze to Roxanne's Country Store across the street. He'd realized this afternoon, as the day was passing and his anticipation at seeing Roxanne again was building, that he hadn't thought to ask where she wanted to go for dinner. While he'd given her his number, he hadn't gotten hers, so here he was gathering his nerve to see her again. He felt silly. She had such a powerful effect on him, he was anxious about doing anything that might cause her to back away. Her wary response to him yesterday gave him pause. He hoped she might still hold a flame in her heart for him, but he didn't really know. His cat growled inside, on the verge of annoyance at the human side of him, which tended to think things through. If his cat had his say, he'd barge into the store now, throw her over his shoulder and find the closest place he could to make her his again.

With a mental shake, he strode across the street and pushed through the swinging door into the store. Diane Franklin, whom he remembered from the many afternoons he spent here years ago, glanced up from the front register. "Hey there, Max! Saw you come in yesterday, but I was busy. How are you?" Diane asked.

Max was so focused on seeing Roxy that he was distracted by Diane's question. He paused and glanced her way. What had she said? Oh right, she asked how he was. "Oh, I'm good. How are you?" He forced himself to be polite. It wouldn't do for him to ignore her just because he wanted to see Roxy. Right now.

Diane smiled, her brown eyes warm. "I'm great. I have two grandkids now. I'm sure you can guess rumor is traveling that you're back here for good. Is that so?"

He nodded. "That's the plan. I missed Catamount the whole time I was gone. After my mom passed away, there was nothing left keeping me in Virginia." He managed to answer politely enough, but he was impatient inside. Roxy was somewhere nearby, and every fiber of him sensed it.

Diane nodded. "I'm sorry to hear about your mother passing. I'm sure you know many of her old friends here would've loved to have seen her again."

"I can imagine. Uh, you don't happen to know if Roxanne is around this afternoon?" He blurted his question out, unable to keep from asking.

Diane's brows hitched up, her eyes assessing. "She's out back. Does she know you're stopping by?"

He shook his head, physically forcing himself to hold still. It wasn't like he worked here. He couldn't exactly storm to the back just because he wanted to. Diane was quiet for a moment after he shook his head, eyeing him thoughtfully. "Well, go on back if you'd like. I'll page her and let her know you're headed her way." She gestured beyond the aisles to a door Max knew led to the storage area of the store. He didn't wait for her to reconsider and strode quickly for the door.

Memories careened through his mind once he stepped into the back hallway. He passed a closed door that he knew led to a small sitting room where he and Roxy used to sneak off and make out whenever they could. It was the only room downstairs that hadn't been completely turned into workspace for the store. Moving past that, he heard motion in what he thought to be the storage room. He turned through the doorway and saw the freezer door open. A pager sat on a table by the door. "Hey girl, Max Stone is here and he's headed your way." Diane's voice came through the small speaker on the pager.

Max eyed the pager and then the massive freezer in the back of the room. He walked toward it. Just as he reached the door with icy air pouring out of it, Roxy stepped through. His breath caught and his pulse lunged, the old, familiar need for her coiling tightly inside. Her blue eyes widened when they landed on him. She stopped where she was. Several locks of her blonde hair had fallen loose from the knot atop her head, held in place with a pen. Her cheeks were rosy from the cold. Everything froze for a moment. Then, with his heart banging hard and fast against his ribs and his longing to touch her so acute, he couldn't hold back.

He closed the distance between them in two long strides. Her head tilted back, and he heard her sharp intake of breath. All he knew was he needed to touch her. He lifted a hand and brushed a lock of hair out of her eyes. "Roxy." Her name came out roughly. His hand moved of its own accord, stroking into her hair, his thumb tracing along her jawline and down onto the soft skin of her neck. Her pulse beat wildly as his touch passed over it. He tried, oh he tried, to hold back, but it was too much to have her this close.

He dipped his head and brought his lips to hers, meaning only to give himself that. But when she sighed against his mouth, he was done for. He fit his mouth over hers and kissed her with everything he had. If she'd tried to stop him, he would have stopped, but she didn't. She held still for a beat before her lips parted. He dove into the warm sweetness of her mouth. He'd been living on memories of her kisses for so long, his knees nearly buckled at how good it felt to actually touch her. When he stroked his tongue into her mouth, hers met his in a sensuous tangle. He stepped closer and slid his hand down her back. At the feel of her luscious curves against him, his cock hardened instantly. He needed her like the air he breathed.

***

Roxanne tumbled into a cauldron of sensation. Max's kiss set her aflame inside. His kiss was better than any she'd remembered with his tongue stroking boldly inside her mouth, tracing her lips, softly nipping and tugging on her bottom lip—essentially driving her wild with desire. She hadn't expected to see him just now, so he'd caught her off guard and undefended. A tiny corner of her mind tried to persuade her she could resist him, but it felt so good, so, so good to be in his arms again, she couldn't stop it.

His lips meandered away from hers, blazing a hot trail of kisses along the column of her throat. The icy air from the freezer drifted around them, a contrast to the fire burning between them. He tugged her close, cupping her bottom with his hand and pulled her against his arousal. She groaned and shifted her hips restlessly. She was so wet, instantly drenched with need, and feeling his hard cock against her nearly undid her. Her hands explored the hard planes of his chest, frantic to re-acquaint herself with every inch of him.

There was a clatter from the deli kitchen down the hall and then the sound of a door opening nearby. Max's teeth closed on the lobe of her ear, sending a prickle along her skin, before he pulled back. She didn't want him to stop and tried to step closer even though she was already plastered against him. His hand moved up her back in a slow pass, coming to rest at her nape where his thumb stroked back and forth in a soft caress.

Their breath heaved, misting in the frosty air surrounding them. She slowly became aware of where they were and what had just happened. She was torn between two impulses—part of her wanted to tear herself from his embrace and run, while another part of her wanted to stay right where she was and never move again. It had been as long as he'd been gone that she'd felt this *right* with someone. She slowly lifted her head—his tawny gaze held hers. Her belly was spinning with flutters and her pulse was galloping wildly.

She shivered in the icy air and finally gathered herself together enough to step back. It almost physically pained her to create any distance between them. His arms slipped off of her as she stepped back, while his eyes remained glued to her.

"Well, I, um…" She paused and blew a puff of air.

"Fifteen years was too long to wait to kiss you again. I missed you," Max said, his voice low and taut.

"I missed you too." Her words escaped on their own, just flew right out without her permission. Her hand clapped over her mouth. Her consternation must've shown on her face because Max shook his head quickly.

"I wouldn't blame you if you didn't want to tell me

you missed me," he said.

His comment only stirred her up because it was just like him to practically read her mind. Once upon a time, she'd loved how well he knew her. Right now, it made her feel too exposed. She felt spun tight inside, caught in the twist and turn of the intense emotions only he could elicit and struggling against the tide of hopes and dreams she'd thought effectively buried rising up with a power she couldn't ignore. She closed her eyes, needing to shield herself from his gaze for a moment. After a few deep breaths, she opened them again and reached back to close the freezer door finally.

"I stopped by to ask where you wanted to meet for dinner. Diane sent me back here," Max said, watching her carefully.

"Oh. Right. Guess we didn't settle on that. Um, how about the Trailhead?"

"Perfect. How about I meet you here and we walk over there?"

Before she could even form a thought, she nodded. Max's smile flashed and her heart squeezed, emotion rolling through her. Back when they were young, Max had been fairly quiet and somber. His smiles were pure and rare. And oh, how she'd missed them! Her own smile spread before she could stop it. When she realized she was standing there smiling like a foolish girl, she shook her head sharply. He seemed to sense her abrupt withdrawal and leaned over to drop a quick kiss on her cheek. "Okay, I'll let you finish up. I'll stop by around six."

At that, he spun around and strode quickly out of the storeroom. Her eyes tracked over him hungrily, savoring the easy swing of his arms, his confident stride and the strength he emanated. When he turned the corner, she took a few steps to lean against the table in the center of the room. Her body was still reverberating from his kiss. She was hot, flustered and drenched with need. She gulped in air and stared at the floor. *Shit, shit, shit. Why did I go and let him kiss me like that? I can't just fall at his feet like a fool. But you wanted to kiss him. Admit it, it felt amazing.*

She squeezed her eyes shut and took a deep breath, desperate to slow her rampaging pulse and ease that sweet wildness he elicited inside of her. He'd always had this strange ability to make her lose her tendency to be guarded and sarcastic. She loved her friends and family dearly, but when it came to men, she'd always had a mildly cynical view. The whole shifter fantasy of mates who were meant to be had seemed like silly yore to her even before Max broke her heart. Then, he'd gone and left her behind, her heart battered and bruised because she'd been stupid enough to let down her guard with him.

Today, he showed up and kissed her, and her silly heart forgot all of that. Once again, she was yearning for him, nostalgia crashing over her in waves. She opened her eyes and sighed. No matter what happened with Max, she still had to finish stocking the shelves.

Chapter 5

With a few hours to go before he could see Roxy again, Max headed down Main Street to the police station. He figured he could ask Hank about his offer to round up some kids to help with yard clean up. He also intended to see what Hank might know about the accident that led to his father's death. The police station was still housed in the same stately brick building as it had been years ago. He climbed the granite steps and entered through the heavy wooden doors, pausing to glance around. The waiting area was quiet with the receptionist on the phone and tapping away at her keyboard. He started to walk toward the counter when a door to the side opened and Hank stepped out.

"Thought I saw you walking up the steps," Hank said with a wide smile. He stepped to Max's side and clapped him on the shoulder. "Have you had a chance to stop by your old place yet?"

"Oh yeah. I stopped by yesterday. That's one reason

I came by. I was hoping maybe you meant it when you said you could round up some kids to help out with the yard clean up."

Hank chuckled, his brown eyes crinkling at the corners in his weathered face. "Of course I meant it. Come on back," he said, opening the door beside him and waving Max through. Hank stepped past him in the hall and turned into an office. "Need some coffee?" he asked, gesturing to a coffee pot on a small table by the doorway.

Max started to shake his head and then shifted into a nod. "Sure. I meant to grab some coffee at Roxanne's earlier, but I forgot."

Hank arched a brow and turned to pour coffee into two paper cups, handing one over to Max before sitting down at a small round table and gesturing for Max to join him. Though Hank had aged in the years Max had been gone, he still held that indefinable sense of strength and power all shifters carried. His brown hair was flecked with gray and his eyes were as perceptive as ever. "Don't quite know how anyone could stop by Roxanne's and forget to get coffee except you. Plain as day that old flame is burning hot and fast between you two. You'd better be ready for rumors to fly. Catamount's grown since you left, but some things never change, especially where gossip is concerned."

Max took a swallow of coffee and glanced over at Hank. "I can deal with it. Just hope Roxy gives me a chance."

Hank nodded slowly. "I've known Roxanne since she was a baby. She's always had a stubborn streak, but she's also got a heart of gold. I'm not privy to how she feels about you, but I know what I saw when she laid eyes on you. Be patient."

Max bit back a sigh. He knew he needed to be patient, but having Roxy this close after so many years of distance made it hard. "I figured I'd need to be. Anyway, back to the house. If you mean it, I could use some serious help cleaning up the yard. The inside of the house is actually in decent shape, just dusty as hell. I'll pay if you can hustle up some help."

"You got it. Give me a few days. Once I tell Gail, she'll spread the word. You planning to move back in?"

"That's the plan."

Hank took a sip of coffee and eyed him. "Heard you took a job as a prosecutor for the county. True?"

"Yup. I would've come back no matter what, but when I saw the position was available, I applied. I don't start until after the holidays. I suppose I'll be seeing plenty of you."

Hank flashed a grin. "That you will." He paused, his gaze sobering. "Your mother reached out to me about your father's accident the year before she passed away. She mentioned she spoke to you about it."

Max's throat tightened, and he took a gulp of coffee. "She did. I was hoping to talk to you about it."

"I'll talk all you want. Problem is it's been fifteen years since your father died in that accident. I wish your mother had called me sooner because the trail's definitely cold. But we've got one thing that might give us some leverage," Hank said.

"What's that?"

"You followed the news up here much?"

"A bit."

"See all those stories about the smuggling ring here and out West?"

Max nodded, his curiosity piqued. He'd seen the stories about the smuggling ring that was splintered here and in a few other shifter communities out West. He'd known shifters must've had something to do with it since several of the Peyton's had been arrested in the aftermath. Wallace Peyton had been the man his mother believed to be behind his father's death. The Peyton family was one of four founding shifter families from centuries gone by. They'd once been revered in the community, so revered that his mother had been terrified to speak out about how his father died and chosen instead to flee the only place they'd ever known as home.

Max caught Hank's gaze. "I saw the news, heard Wallace and Randall got arrested, but I don't know what that has to do with anything."

"Just that they're locked up and we might get one of them to talk. You're a prosecutor, you know the deal. They can cut all kinds of deals to reduce their sentence for good behavior. Cooperating with other investigations is one of them. Not to mention, Brad Peyton managed to keep his nose just clean enough to strike a deal and get released early. Of the lot of 'em, he was the only Peyton who felt guilty about what the family brought down on shifters. I've got no trouble leaning on him. The investigation is still technically open and probably will be for a while. The feds got involved once we confirmed the crimes occurred across state lines."

"Yeah, but it's not like Wallace is going to fess up about being involved in my father's death and what would his sons know about it?" Max asked.

Hank shrugged. "So maybe Wallace won't fess up, but his back is against the wall as it is. I figure we rattle his cage. As for Randall and Brad, you'd be surprised what they might know. How about you fill me in on what you know and I'll start poking around?"

"I wish I knew more. All I know is my mother said my dad became aware Wallace was embezzling profits at the mill. When he started trying to figure out who to tell

about it, he died. The same day he died, she got a call from
Wallace to give his condolences about my father. She said it
was crazy because he called before anyone else knew my
father died, including her. She later found out he called
before my dad actually died. The only reason she didn't call
you sooner was because it was five years before she got
around to getting his official autopsy report. That's when
she realized Wallace's call came a little bit before my
father's accident. That's all I know."

Hank's brows hitched up. "No wonder she got
suspicious. Well, I'll start digging. You'll need to be
patient. I don't want to stir the waters so fast that people
start shutting down. I figure if your father was suspicious
about Wallace's smuggling, he probably wasn't the only
one. Give me some time, and I'll see what I can do."

Max took a deep breath and let it out in a sigh.
"Well, it's been fifteen years. I can wait. I didn't even know
about all this until about a year ago. Finally helped me
realize why my mom was so determined we had to leave
right away." He took another gulp of coffee, draining the
small cup and leaned back in his chair. "I'm just glad
you're willing to take a look after all this time."

"No question on that. Your family meant a lot to this
community. If Wallace was behind what happened, I want
to know. Don't go thinking the Peyton's are what they once
were around here. They put all shifters at risk with their
scheme to use shifters for smuggling drugs. They're almost
shunned around here now," Hank explained.

"The news didn't mention anything about shifters. I
just figured Wallace was looking for another way to make
money."

Hank rolled his eyes. "Of course the news didn't
mention shifters. We're not the only police department that
knows how to protect our own. That detail wasn't relevant

to anyone other than shifters. But yeah, that's why most of Catamount shifters despise the once high and mighty Peyton's. Wallace sold shifters to the highest bidder. He got a line to some guys out West that were just as happy to put us all at risk." Hank paused and shook his head sharply, bitterness flashing in his eyes. "Man makes me sick, but it's okay. We broke the ring up. Sad thing is, it's still not like it once was. There're a few shifters who were probably involved and somehow avoided detection." Hank shrugged. "All we can do is hope they've learned their lesson at this point."

Max leaned back in his chair, shock rippling through him. "Damn. I knew Wallace was an asshole, but I've never have guessed he'd put shifters at risk like that."

"I wish I could say I was surprised, but Wallace was always after two things: power and money. If it hadn't been for his family's history, he likely never would've gotten to where he did. Such an arrogant jerk," Hank said with a shake of his head. "Anyway, enough of that. I'll start dusting things off on that investigation. Check in anytime. You'll see me around plenty if you're stopping by Roxanne's."

Max nodded. "Thanks again." He stood from his chair with Hank rising to his feet at the same time. When he reached the door to the station, he glanced back to Hank who'd followed him quietly. For a moment, anger rose swiftly inside. He was only here asking for Hank to look into his father's death because he had to. If Wallace Peyton had somehow orchestrated his father's death, Max had to know the truth. He caught Hank's eyes. "Before I go, here's my number. You can call me if you have any luck rounding up some clean up help for me." Max quickly recited his number.

"Oh, it won't be luck. If you're paying, there's

plenty of kids who'll be happy to help," Hank said with a chuckle as he entered Max's number in his phone.

Max gave a wave and left, pausing by the sidewalk to look up and down the familiar street. It was strange to return to Catamount. This place was the only place that had ever felt like home, yet it was so odd to actually be here after so many years of nothing but memories. His eyes traced the roofline of Roxanne's Country Store several blocks away from here. The place was the same magnet it had once been—all because the woman who held his heart in her hands was there.

***

Roxanne stood inside her bathroom and stared in the mirror. She hadn't given her appearance much thought in the last few years. But now she was going to dinner with Max, and it suddenly mattered how she looked. Her blonde hair was almost always in a knot, usually held in place with whatever pen or pencil she happened upon when she needed it. With her busy life, she needed to keep her hair out of her eyes. She lifted a hand and tugged the pencil free. Her long, blonde hair fell in loose waves around her shoulders. She grabbed a brush and dragged it through her hair. Spinning away from the mirror, she strode into her bedroom and stared in the closet. She had absolutely no idea what to wear, although she should probably get a grip and wear whatever she might normally wear to dinner at The Trailhead Café. The Trailhead was best described as dinner casual. It garnered its name from Catamount's location near the Appalachian Trail, the long winding trail through the Appalachian Mountains, which ran from Georgia to Maine. Hikers trekked through Catamount from early spring to late autumn in their quest to complete the trail. Roxanne ate there frequently with friends as it was a fixture in town and served reliably good food. She couldn't recall a single time she'd thought much about what to wear.

She spun away from her closet and sat down on her bed with a sigh. She looked around the room and wondered what it meant that she still lived in her childhood home. Aside from Max, she'd never had a relationship serious enough to consider another life. She loved running her family's old store and loved Catamount. Being a shifter meant managing risk. Staying in the oldest known shifter community offered her the ability to live as who she was without too much fear. Yet, here she was in the same home where she'd been born. The upstairs of the store was like the many colonial homes scattered throughout New England. Tall ceilings and windows, gleaming hardwood floors and large rooms made up the home. After her parents had passed away, she'd eventually relocated into the master bedroom, mainly because she liked the massive bathroom with its stunning old claw foot tub.

She took a deep breath and stood. Dammit, she would not obsess over what to wear. She'd just get dressed like usual. Moments later, she walked downstairs. She wove through the center aisle, tossing a grin Diane's way as she passed by, and pushed through the front door. The bell chimed softly behind her just as she glanced up to see Max crossing the street. The setting sun glinted off his mahogany hair. His eyes met hers across the street. Her breath caught. It felt as if a flame lit up and danced through the air between them.

Chapter 6

Max looked across the table at Roxy. Her gaze lifted and caught his, her blue eyes bright in the soft lighting. He yearned for the way things once felt between them—easy and comfortable with an ever-present hum of desire surrounding them. The desire was still as strong as it had ever been, yet she held herself at an invisible distance. He'd hoped after their unexpected kiss the other day that perhaps her reserve had eased. Instead, he sensed she was reacting against the kiss. He could feel how guarded she was, and he hated it. They'd managed to get through the walk from the store to here with nothing but superficial conversation. Their waitress had taken their order and served a bottle of wine. He pondered how quickly to cut to the chase. The lion within him was nearly lunging against the restraint.

"Roxy, can you give me a chance to explain?" he asked abruptly.

She looked at him for a long moment before taking a sip of wine. With a flick of her hand, she brushed her tousled blonde hair behind her shoulder before nodding. Her eyes were clear with a hint of a challenge in them.

"It's not like I have any great excuse, but I was just numb and not thinking straight the day my dad died. I got home and my mom had already packed up the house. Next thing I knew, we were driving to Virginia to stay with my aunt. My mom told me we wouldn't be returning to Catamount. I didn't know why at the time, but she was also freaked out about us staying in touch with anyone. I couldn't even think straight, so when I called you, I honestly thought I would never see you again." He paused and swallowed against the constricted feeling in his chest and throat. It hurt to think about how surreal the first few weeks had been after his father died.

He looked across at Roxy to see her eyes were glimmering with tears, but she didn't look away and simply stared at him. He took a deep breath and plowed ahead. He'd promised himself he'd lay it on the line with her so she knew exactly where he stood. "I never stopped loving you and I've missed you every day since we left. By the time I could think halfway clearly, I tried to call, but your mom was pretty pissed off with me. The thing I didn't understand back then was why my mom was so insistent we had to leave. I don't have all the details because she didn't, but she thought Wallace Peyton had my father killed. I don't know how, but my dad thought Wallace was embezzling from the mill where my dad worked. Back then, Wallace Peyton pretty much ran this town. I talked to Hank today and…"

Roxy set her wineglass down with a thunk, cutting into his words, her eyes wide and her mouth falling open. "Are you serious?"

"Well, yeah. That's why my mom took off and was so determined to keep us away from Catamount. I didn't know why until about a year before she passed away. By then, it seemed like it might be way too late to try to explain." He paused and held her gaze. "I never forgot you. I came back because I wanted to have a chance again. I just hope you'll give it to me."

Roxy tore her eyes from his and looked down at the table, tracing her fingertip in a circle around the base of her wineglass. She was quiet for so long, Max worried he'd pushed too far and too fast. "I'm so sorry about your dad," she said softly. "You were close to him."

Max still missed his father, but he'd come to terms with the loss as best he could. "I was. I still miss him, but I'm okay. I asked Hank to open an investigation into his death. He said he would. He thinks with everything that's gone down with the Peyton's that we might have a chance to get somewhere with it."

She still didn't meet his eyes, her finger circling the wineglass slowly. "I don't know what to do with you showing up like this," she finally said.

Max's mind spun as he tried to think of the right thing to say that would persuade her of what he knew to be true—they were meant to be together and no one called to him the way she did. "Roxy," he said, his voice roughened with the edges of his feelings.

Her shoulders rose and fell with a breath before she lifted her gaze to his. The pain he saw in the depths of her eyes sliced right through him. He might have all kinds of reasons why he hadn't had enough sense to handle things differently back then, but it didn't change how much he'd hurt her. Which nearly killed him inside. He'd gone and hurt the person who meant more to him than anyone. She was quiet, her eyes scanning his face. She blinked, drawing attention to the sheen of tears. He reached over and gripped her hand.

"I blew it. Big time. Even if I was young and not really with it after my dad died, I should've found a way to call you sooner. I was just, well, I was in shock. By the time I wasn't, my mom was pretty pushy about me not contacting anyone from Catamount. But none of that changes the fact I hurt you. We were lucky, so damn lucky to find each other when we were that young, and I hurt you. I'm so damn sorry."

He squeezed her hand and felt a subtle squeeze from her, which sent hope soaring inside. He was clinging to the hope they'd find a way past the chasm his abrupt departure and time and distance had created. He heard her breath come out slowly as she lifted her chin, a hint of her strength showing. "It was awful when you left, but the worst part was I was worried about you and I couldn't even talk to you." A tear rolled down her cheek and she swiped at it quickly, tugging her hand free from his. "I didn't know any of this stuff about Wallace and your dad. I wish I had because it makes sense why your mom wouldn't want to be here." She paused and shook her head sharply. "Anyway, that's another thing altogether. As for us…I just need some time. I can't tell how I really feel right now. It's all too much."

He forced himself to breathe. He'd reminded himself probably a thousand times that he had no idea if he could ever have a chance with Roxanne again. The miracle that she wasn't out of his reach needed to be enough now. "I understand."

She nodded slowly. "Okay." After a quiet moment, she nodded. "How about we try to be normal? You know, have dinner, catch up, that kind of thing." A wry smile lifted one corner of her mouth, and his heart gave a hard thump.

"Normal sounds good."

Their waitress conveniently arrived to deliver their food. Max grinned when Roxanne quickly dug into her meal. She loved to cook and she loved to eat. That meant plenty of amazing meals for him when they were together. Even at seventeen, she'd been well on her way to becoming a phenomenal chef. The Trailhead Café served dinners from casual to more fancy. Roxanne had gone with a creamy fettuccini dish with smoked salmon, while he'd opted for a burger.

Starting to eat snapped the tension lingering from their serious conversation and Max managed to shift it onto more casual terrain. "So how long have you been running the store on your own?"

"Officially about five years. My dad passed away after complications from pneumonia. My mom had a stoke the year before that, so she was already in a nursing home then."

"I'm sorry to hear that. I bet you miss them," Max cut in quickly. Roxanne's family had been tight, so he knew it must've been hard for her after they passed.

She caught his eyes for a second before nodding and swirling her fork in the fettuccini. "Thanks. It's okay. Time is what it is. I was just glad my mom didn't while away too long in the nursing home. She'd have hated that. She passed within six months of him. Then, it was just me. I suppose I'm technically the one in charge, but Diane runs the front like she did before, and I have plenty of help. But you know what I do. What about you?" she asked with a slight smile.

"I'm an attorney. I was a prosecutor in Virginia, and I took a job here for the county. I start after the holidays. I'd always meant to come back, but I was never sure about the timing because I didn't want to leave my mother on her own. After she passed away, I started the process of selling her house down there and getting ready to move. The county prosecutor position opened up here, and I took the chance. I'd have come with or without a job, but it made the move easier knowing I had work lined up."

Roxanne finished chewing and took a sip of wine before looking over at him, a smile stretching across her face. "That's the perfect job for you! You always loved to make sure things were fair, and you were always investigating one thing after another."

His smile spread from within. He was pleased beyond measure to have Roxanne think anything like that, not because the details mattered, but because it told him she remembered him and knew him at his core. They sat like that for several long moments, grinning at each other across the table, before their waitress arrived.

"How are we doing here? Need anything?" the waitress asked. She paused and glanced between them, her dark eyes assessing. "Well, the rumors are certainly true," she commented.

Roxanne glanced up to her. "What do you mean?"

The waitress shrugged, her dark ponytail swinging a little with the motion. "You're Max Stone, right?" she asked.

At his nod, she continued. "Everyone says you two were totally in love back in the day. You know how it is around here," she offered, referencing the lore around shifters finding their true mates. Max would've guessed she was a shifter solely based on the way she carried herself. "Not everyone finds each other. Anyway, I saw the way you were just looking at each other, and it's pretty obvious."

Max held his breath, worried the innocent observation would set Roxanne on edge. She surprised him with a shrug before she took another sip of wine. "Dinner's delicious, as always," she finally replied, deflecting quickly from the topic.

He was so relieved she didn't get defensive at the waitress's comment that his breath came out in a rush. The waitress glanced between them. "If you don't need anything else, I'll bring the check." At his nod, she started to turn away and then glanced back, her eyes flicking from him to Roxanne. "Don't let it slip away. Not everyone gets this kind of chance." At that, she spun around.

Roxanne's mouth fell open. With her eyes wide, she swung her gaze to him. "Wow, she's got some nerve. In case you were wondering, the gossip mill here is as bad as it ever was," she said with a roll of her eyes.

He shrugged. "Catamount wouldn't be the same without it."

***

Roxanne walked beside Max down Main Street. It was early November and the streets had been decorated for the holidays with lights hanging merrily along the streets and homes. Catamount, like so many small towns in New England, was almost postcard perfect during the holidays with its stately old homes, tree lined streets and small parks scattered through town. The town green in the center of town had a stunning Balsam fir that rose tall in the middle of the granite paths crisscrossing the green. The holiday lights glittered on it in the darkness.

Max's palm rested at her waist. She wasn't sure when he'd placed it here, but the warmth of his touch seared her. With everything he'd said tonight, it was all she could do not to fling herself into his arms. She wanted so desperately to believe he meant what he said. Yet, the scars from her pain and grief after he left were deep. For over fifteen years, she'd built up the walls around her heart because she couldn't imagine letting herself be as vulnerable as she had with Max. Not knowing why he hadn't tried to stay connected after he moved away left her to come to the only conclusion she could at the time—he hadn't loved her the way she thought he had.

His rejection had cut her to her core. She'd loved him so completely, and she'd regretted it for years. The habits of protection ran deep. Everything he said about why he'd broken it off with her made sense. She needed time to sort through it. She wasn't even sure she could trust her own heart right now. Perhaps the overwhelming connection she felt to him was only nostalgia and those lingering wishes he'd come back to her. With a mental shake, she brought her mind back to the moment with Max's hand warm on her back and the chilly air of the impending winter easing the heat inside.

They walked quietly through the night, leaves crunching under their footsteps. When they reached the store, she slid the key into the lock and opened the door. Before she thought about it, she spoke. "Do you want some coffee?"

He nodded, his warm tawny gaze holding hers. Flustered, she gestured for him to follow her. Once he stepped inside, she closed the door behind him. They walked through the darkened aisles in the front of the store. Memories assailed her of so many late evenings here with him, sneaking kisses whenever they could find a moment alone. She pushed through the door to the deli kitchen and headed behind the counter with Max following her. He leaned against the table in the center of the kitchen while she quickly prepped espressos for them. The quiet between them was comfortable and made her want to forget her silly worries.

She slid his mug to him and shimmied her hips onto the table beside him, swinging her legs restlessly once she was seated. A sip of the dark brew she'd prepped gave her a dose of clarity. This was nothing more than coffee with an old boyfriend. She could do this.

Max angled towards her, the low light from the front catching on his mahogany hair. "We're doing okay with normal," he said, a smile hooking one corner of his mouth.

In a flash, the air around them heated. Her low belly clenched and her pulse lunged. He set his coffee down and turned more fully to face her. Everything blurred, need sliding through her veins like fire. He moved slowly, as if giving her the opportunity to stop him, but she couldn't have. She yearned for his touch so deeply, it was a need she couldn't deny. He lifted a hand and brushed her hair off her shoulder, his hand curling around the nape of her neck. Caught in his gaze of honeyed fire, she couldn't look away and could barely breathe.

He took a step and stood between her knees. Heat and strength emanated from him. Emotion, longing and pure desire washed through her, suffusing her inside and out. His eyes searched her face. Her breath escaped in a sigh. He angled his head to the side and dropped a kiss at the corner of her brow. From there, he dusted kisses along her cheek and to the edge of her jawline where the feel of his breath against her skin sent shivers racing through her. He made his way to her mouth. By the time his lips reached hers, she was near frantic with need. He teased her with soft kisses and traced her lips with his tongue before he fit his mouth over hers. One bold stroke of his tongue and she moaned into his mouth. She slipped her hands around his waist and tugged him to her, curling her legs around his hips. The moment his hard shaft pressed against her core, their kiss went wild. Licks, strokes, nips and a sensuous tangle of tongues.

Pure need roared through her. It had been so damn long since she'd let herself go with anyone. As long as it had been since she'd last been with Max. She wanted him like she'd never wanted anyone. To have him here, his hands roaming over her and that wild thrumming passion burning her up inside, was almost more than she could bear. As long as it didn't stop. A tiny voice tried to raise its resistance. The burning need inside shouted it down.

She shoved his jacket off his shoulders and yanked at his shirt. She needed to feel his skin. While she flung his clothes to the floor, he made quick work of hers. She sighed when she stroked a palm over the hard planes of his chest. He cupped her breasts, her name coming out with a groan. She meant to tug him against her, but before she could, he dipped his head and swirled his tongue around a nipple.

She completely forgot what she meant to do and tumbled into a cauldron of sensation. He traced circles around her nipples and lightly pinched them before drawing one and then the other into his mouth. Amidst pants and gasps, she fumbled with his jeans and slid a hand over his briefs to stroke his cock. She savored his groan when he tore his lips from her breast and looked up. His eyes locked with hers, and it was just like she remembered—nothing but the two of them and this wild, intense feeling beating like a drum between them. The connection she had with him was like no other.

Holding her gaze, he curled his hands around her hips and dragged her to the edge of the table. She was drenched with desire, her panties nearly soaked. She lost track of exploring him when he swiftly unbuttoned her jeans and lifted her hips just enough the drag them down. She kicked them free, her heart pounding so hard and fast, she couldn't think of anything other than finally being as close to him as she needed. He dragged a finger back and forth over the black silk between her legs. Her channel tightened in anticipation.

"Max…don't wait…" she choked out.

He shoved the silk out of the way and stroked his fingers into her folds. Her hips shifted restlessly. One finger and then another slid inside of her. She closed her eyes, savoring every subtle stroke of his fingers. She was so close, so damn close to release. Her eyes flew open when he dragged his fingers out.

"I have to be inside you when you come." His words were rough, coming out in between his heaving breath.

She reached for him, shoving his jeans and briefs down around his hips. She started to yank him to her, but he held back, fumbling in his pocket and pulling his wallet out. In seconds, he tore open the foil packet and rolled a condom on. The interruption served only to amp up her need. Frantic, she curled her legs around his hips. He paused, the head of his cock resting at her entrance.

"Roxy, look at me."

She looked up into his fiery gaze. After a several beats, he sank into her slowly, his eyes on her the entire time. When he was seated fully within her, he held still and stroked a hand through her hair. "I missed you so much," he whispered.

She nodded, emotion and desire a wild tangle inside. "I missed you too. So much." The bare truth escaped in the depth of the intimate moment.

Max started to move in slow strokes, driving deeply each time. She gasped at the stretch of him filling her, sweet pleasure curling inside. Again and again, he brought her closer and closer. She toed the edge of her delicious release over and over and over again. He slipped a hand between them and circled it over the center of her desire, and she tumbled over the edge. Her orgasm crashed through her in waves as he tightened against her and cried out roughly, his head whipping back and then falling forward, his forehead resting against hers.

With soft shudders rolling through her, Roxanne slowly relaxed in Max's embrace. She couldn't quite believe what had just happened. Even though a part of her was wondering just what the hell she'd gone and done, most of her knew she couldn't have turned away from this. Her cat most emphatically approved of giving in to the pounding, pulsing desire between her and Max. He slowly lifted his head, and she opened her eyes. His palm slid up her back in a slow pass, coming to rest between her shoulder blades, his thumb stroking idly. Her heart split wide open under his gaze. She swallowed and took a breath.

"I, um… Well, that just happened," she said, her words raspy.

His eyes searched her face before the corner of his mouth kicked up. "It did," he said, the low timbre of his voice sending a shiver through her.

Chapter 7

Max watched Roxy, wishing he could climb inside her mind to see what she was thinking. Her blue eyes were luminous in the faint light. He hadn't expected this…at all. Yet, when he'd looked at her and seen her glance over, the guarded look in her eyes gone, his primal need had taken control. The moment he kissed her, he was lost. Her skin was warm against him. When she took a breath, her lush breasts rose against his chest and lust jolted him. Again. It wasn't enough that he'd finally, finally been skin to skin with her. He figured it would be a good long time before his need for her would be slaked.

She held his gaze for several breaths before her eyes fell. She lifted a hand and traced along his collarbone. When she looked up again, she looked resigned. "I didn't expect this," she said softly.

"I didn't either."

He waited, trying to keep from filling the silence. He knew Roxy didn't handle pressure well, so no matter how much he wanted to point out that what lay between them was as powerful as it had ever been, he held back.

She bit her lip and let her hand fall. "Well, I suppose it was inevitable."

"What was inevitable?"

"This," she replied, gesturing between them. "I don't know what it means."

He started to reply, but held back. His lion nearly roared within. The primal side of him knew the plain truth —Roxy was meant to be his and always had. He simply had to wait until she saw the truth as clearly as he did, until she had enough time to believe in him again. It took just about all of his discipline, but he managed to sound reasonable. "To me, it means what it always did. I love you in every way that matters. Fifteen years of missing you piled up inside." Her eyes widened at his words, but she was quiet. "I can wait until you figure out what it means to you," he finally said.

Her blue eyes held his for several beats before she nodded. "I just need some time."

Given that he'd barreled through so many barriers between them, he could be patient even though it strained his willpower.

**

Roxanne stood alone in the living room upstairs. She spun in a slow circle, her eyes traveling along the tall windows with light spilling through them, following the clean lines of the room with its dark oak flooring and bright white walls. She'd gone through a burst of cleaning a few years back and gotten rid of many of her parents' old possessions, keeping only a few mementos that mattered to her, along with some of the antiques that had been passed down through generations. After that, she'd ruthlessly cleaned the upper portion of the home that contained her family's living quarters and the store. She'd needed it to feel like a fresh start even if she was in the very same place she'd been born and raised.

Max's return was stirring her up in so many ways. She was once again dreaming about a life with him. In the heady days of their young love, they'd hatched fanciful plans of building their own home in a small valley just outside of town. Even though she'd missed him like crazy and had to plow through letting go of her dreams, she hadn't resented taking over her family's store and staying in her childhood home. Catamount was home. Her family had been here for centuries and had been one of the founding shifter families. Pride and lore ran deep within her. Her cat rustled inside to think about possibilities again.

It was hard to beat back the hope unfurling within, yet her heart was uncertain. What if Max was only overcome with nostalgia for what once was? How could they even know if their silly young love would ever have gone anywhere? Her heart had felt shredded with pain in the months after he left, and she'd never quite been able to put him behind her. With him here now, overwhelming in the flesh, she could hardly think, much less have a clear idea of how to handle any of it. She closed her eyes and took a breath, remembering the feel of him sheathing himself inside of her. Her pulse skipped and heat slid through her at the memory. She gave her head a shake and opened her eyes.

She needed to get to work. This morning happened to be a late morning for her. Usually she was the first one in the deli, but twice a week she started later to give herself time to work on ordering, accounting and whatever else she needed to catch up on. She'd tossed and turned last night after her interlude with Max in the kitchen. Her mind had tied itself in knots over worry about what it all meant. After she finally fell asleep, her sleep had been interrupted with fevered dreams of him.

As she made her way downstairs, she hoped for a busy day. She could use something to keep her mind off Max and to make her feel halfway normal. Once she pushed through the door into the deli, she was swept up.

Becky glanced over from the register where a line wound from the counter to the aisles. "Oh, thank God you're here! It's been nuts since we opened. I forgot today was the Harvest Fest."

Roxanne glanced through the aisles to Main Street, which was filled with people milling about on the town green. Leaves fluttered in the air, creating a festive atmosphere. She'd been so absorbed in thinking about Max she'd tuned out the low hum of conversation from the street. She caught Becky's eyes and grinned. "Me too. Well, I'm here now."

She snagged an apron off a hook on the wall and strode to Becky's side. "You want me to spell you here, or help Joey over there?"

Becky handed change over to the customer waiting at the front of the line before glancing to Roxanne. "If you don't mind taking over here, I'll help him."

"Not a problem," Roxanne replied, slipping in front of the register when Becky stepped away and headed to a counter towards the back where Joey was busy preparing various breakfast orders.

The hours flew by. Roxanne served so many coffees, she was practically dizzy from spinning back and forth between the register to espresso machine. Meanwhile, Joey and Becky admirably worked like mad, making sandwich after sandwich for the rush of customers coming in from the chilly autumn morning. With Thanksgiving right around the corner, winter was blowing in as the leaves blew loose from the trees. Catamount had an annual gathering, simply named the Harvest Fest, for local farmers to sell off the last of their harvest in anticipation of winter. The event brought hordes of locals and tourists to the area.

By the time closing rolled around, she was exhausted. She leaned against the counter and rolled her head from side to side to ease the tension. Joey turned on the dishwasher and strolled to the front of the deli. Becky had already taken off a few minutes prior.

"I'll be in first thing tomorrow, okay?" Joey asked as he ran a hand through his shaggy brown hair.

Roxanne tossed a weary smile his way. "Perfect. Thanks for working your butt off today."

Joey shrugged. "No problem. It's what you pay me to do."

"So true. But not everyone works as hard as you do, so thanks anyway. Now get outta here."

Joey threw a grin over his shoulder as he headed past the counter. He was all arms and legs and seemed to grow an inch by the day. She turned and watched him walk down the aisle, his lanky form casting a long shadow in the darkened store. The bell chimed as he left. She heard footsteps approach the door again and the distinct sound of the lock clicking in place. The footsteps moved in her direction, and she saw Diane corner the center aisle and make her way toward the deli.

"Hey there. You look as tired as I feel. Crazy day, huh?" Diane asked with a weary smile.

"Oh yeah. No complaints though. I just wish I'd remembered what day it was. I'd have come down earlier."

Diane reached her and hitched one hip on the counter beside Roxanne. A gleam entered her eyes. "Any reason you spaced it?"

Roxanne knew Diane was referring to Max's sudden reappearance in her world. She rolled her eyes and shrugged. "Maybe so." She eyed the floor, visually counting the hardwood slats. She glanced to Diane and summoned her nerve. She was tossed and turned by Max and didn't know which way was up. She could use some advice, and she trusted Diane completely. "We had dinner last night. He, uh, said he never stopped missing me and he wants a chance again. I don't even know what to think."

Diane angled her head to the side. "Well, thinking won't do you much good. How do you feel?"

Roxanne threw her hands up. "Half-crazy! How do you think I feel? You know how I was about him back then. I was all kinds of crazy in love. But we were just seventeen. How can I trust anything I felt back then? Then he shows up out of the blue, and it's like my heart's boomeranged back in time."

Diane's eyes crinkled with her soft smile. "Sweetie, we're all half crazy when we're seventeen, but it doesn't mean what you felt wasn't real. Did he say anything about what happened?"

"Oh yeah. To make a long story short, his mom got them the hell out of here because she was afraid Wallace Peyton had something to do with Max's dad's accident. I guess his father found out Wallace was embezzling from the mill. That was back when Wallace was mayor and threw his weight around town left and right. I gotta say, I was relieved he was arrested after that whole smuggling mess, but it's been nice not having to deal with the cocky Peyton's anymore. You'd think they were the only founding family in this whole damn town."

Diane rolled her eyes and chuckled. "Yeah, that's been a nice side benefit to the Peyton's getting knocked off their pedestal. Anyway, back to Max. Are you serious?!"

she asked, her eyes wide. "If that really happened, no wonder his mom dragged them out of here as fast as she did. Honestly, even if she was just worried about it, the way Wallace was back then, anyone else would've done the same thing."

"I know. It makes the whole thing make more sense. Max said he was just so shocked about everything, he wasn't thinking clearly. It's not that that's got me all mixed up, it's just trying to figure out what's real now. Maybe he's all caught up in nostalgia, maybe I am. I mean, he walked through that door," she paused to gesture to the front of the store "and it's like a tornado in my life. I was all settled down. I didn't have any personal drama in my life, and I was totally good with that. I don't need this, but here he is anyway and I don't know what the hell to do about it!"

Diane was quiet for a long moment and then she leaned over and gave Roxanne a quick hug. "Just because things were good the way they were doesn't mean change isn't good. Maybe Max came out of nowhere, but you wouldn't be all stirred up like this if he didn't matter. Maybe you should try to stop thinking so damn hard and just play it by ear."

"Play it by ear?" Roxanne asked, anxiety knotting in her chest and clenching her gut. She felt like she was spinning inside, emotions rolling in circles and throwing her off balance. "I don't like to play things by ear. I like to plan and know what's going to happen. I like to be in control, dammit!"

Diane arched a brow. "You are most definitely your mother's daughter through and through. She liked to run everything. Thing is, that's not always how things go. If you ask me, I've been wondering when you might actually notice a man. It's kind of overdue. The way I see it, if Max still makes you sit up and take notice, then you might want to pay attention. If it's just nostalgia, it'll wear off pretty fast. If I was a betting woman, I'd bet against nostalgia though."

"Did you forget how much I hate getting advice?" Roxanne asked, exasperated with Diane's encouragement to 'play it by ear.'

"Definitely not, but I'm almost old enough to be your mother, so I get to give it," Diane offered with a wide smile.

Roxanne rolled her eyes and laughed before sobering quickly. "I'm not too good at playing anything by ear." She had to swallow against the tightness in her throat as she considered Max and the tidal wave of emotion he'd brought into her life.

Chapter 8

Max stood on the porch at his childhood home and watched while a swarm of high school kids, boys and girls alike, spread around the yard. Hank had gone above and beyond in his recruiting for a yard clean up crew. He'd called Max late yesterday to report he'd meet him at the house this morning. The kids showed up in batches after Hank and immediately got to work under his direction, raking leaves, pulling up clusters of weeds, clearing out brush everywhere, and basically working like mad. Hank helped coach several of the sports teams at the high school. Between him and his wife, they'd rounded up close to twenty kids. Hank seemed to view this as another coaching job and had immediately stepped in to direct the action after he clarified from Max what he wanted done.

Max took a long swallow of the coffee he'd picked up at Roxanne's Country Store this morning. He'd been disappointed to find she was tied up out back with a delivery when he stopped by, but he'd happily gotten his coffee before driving to meet Hank here. He stepped off the porch and strode across the yard to Hank's side.

"You outdid yourself today. Thanks for rounding these kids up," Max said when he reached Hank.

Hank flashed a grin and adjusted his worn Red Sox baseball cap. "Once I mentioned you were paying, it was a stampede," he replied with a chuckle.

"They'll have this place cleaned up way faster than I could've, that's for sure."

As he scanned the yard, he could now see his mother's old flowerbeds, stripped bare of piled up brush and weeds. The pattern of the slate walkways meandering about the yard was becoming visible again. Hank called out something to a group of boys yanking on a cluster of vines and turned back to Max. "I pulled up the old file on your father's accident. I wasn't the Chief of Police back then, but I was on the force. I don't think they even assigned an investigator. My guess is that was Wallace pulling strings. Catamount police have always covered River Run because the town isn't much more than its mill."

Max took another gulp of coffee and forced himself to breathe slowly. He'd believed he'd gotten beyond the loss of his father, but the past year had cast that into question. He supposed it was mostly because ever since he'd found out about his mother's suspicions, he wanted answers. If his father's death was something more than a random accident, he wanted to know. "Anything of note in there?" he finally asked.

Hank turned to face Max, his eyes considering. "Hard to say. It's a basic accident report. How much did your mother tell you about the accident?"

Max realized Hank might be trying to shield him from the details. "I think she told me everything she knew. She waited until I was little older and then saved her suspicions about Wallace until she got sick. As for what I know about the accident itself, she told me a piece of equipment failed and he was pulled into the rollers. That's it." Paper mills like the one his father worked at had massive rollers that flattened and compressed large swathes of pulp into paper. Accidents such as his father's weren't uncommon in paper mills, even in the modern era.

Hank nodded slowly. "That's what the report said. The detail missing is which equipment failed and how something like that caused him to get in caught the rollers. Funny how when you read about an accident, you notice what's missing if you're looking. I'm not holding it against whoever responded to the accident, but it seems like an obvious question. I've got a list of employees who were present at the time of the accident and plan to follow up with all of them. Fifteen years seems like a long time, but it's not too much in the big scheme. Everyone who was there is still alive today. I'm thinking if your father suspected Wallace was embezzling, it's likely others did too. River Run Mill closed down about five years after that, but almost everyone is still around."

Max absorbed Hank's words. "It sounds like you think you have a few ways to look into this?"

Hank nodded firmly, his confidence clear. "Definitely. In this case, time is our friend. Until last year when Wallace finally got arrested for his role in the smuggling ring, not many people would've felt comfortable trying to stand up to him. Now he's behind bars. It's not like he had much goodwill to coast on anyway. Founding family or not, shifters were damn sick of him throwing his weight around. His sons were just as bad. You heard Callen died, right?"

Max nodded. "Yeah, saw that on the news. Didn't realize it was all tangled up in the smuggling mess here."

Hank shook his head ruefully. "I'm damn relieved that's over, but it cast a pall over Catamount, especially shifters. The Peyton name is hardly spoken around here anymore. With that, we might get somewhere if anyone knows anything about your dad's accident."

A bracing gust of wind blew a pile of leaves in a swirl. Max took a deep breath of the chilly air and looked out over the yard, recalling autumns gone by when he'd help his father clean up before the snow came. He glanced back to Hank. "Thanks for looking into this. I know you don't have to."

Hank looked at him for a long moment. "Of course. Far as I'm concerned, there's no question I'd look into it." He paused when two boys passed by, their arms filled with vines bunched together. "Good work on those. Those vines don't make it easy," he commented. They boys grinned and kept walking to the area Max had identified for a burn pile. They tossed the brush on the pile and immediately headed back to the corner of the yard where they'd been working.

Hours later, Max watched Hank's truck pull away in the fading light. The kids had largely finished the job in one day. Max slowly walked around the perimeter of the yard. The stone wall was completely cleared of the overgrown bushes and weeds. The entire area was cleared of leaves. His mother had loved gardening and the yard was scattered with flowerbeds with slate walkways weaving through them. There were no flowers now and hadn't been for years, but at least he could see where they should be. When he reached the cluster of trees where his old tree house had been, he glanced up. He'd helped a few kids tear down the last remnants of the tree house. There was nothing left anymore except his memories. He spun to look at the house. The ivy had been torn down, along with the vines creeping along the porches. The dangling shutters were neatly stacked on the back porch.

He walked up the steps and turned to look toward the mountains. The sun had fallen below the horizon within the last hour, leaving a watercolor sky behind as darkness slowly took over. His lion rumbled inside. He'd become so accustomed to rarely shifting, he hadn't shifted since he'd been back home. Aside from everything else he'd had to adjust to when they moved abruptly away from Catamount, he'd had to learn that the secrecy protecting shifters was nearly absolute outside of Catamount. For fifteen years, he'd had to shackle his lion inside and learn to live with it because it wasn't safe to shift outside of the wilderness. Just now, his lion nearly roared to be free. In the safety of Catamount and along the edges of the mountains, Max shifted and let his lion run free for the first time in years.

Power surged through him in an intense wave. Fur rippled across his skin and he leapt off the porch, bounding into the woods behind the house. He traversed through the foothills, moving with sureness and swiftness. Fifteen years may have passed, but his lion clearly remembered these woods and mountains. He wove through the trees in the darkening forest until he was climbing higher and higher, the ground becoming rocky. The release of letting his lion run free echoed deep within him. He savored the strength and power of every leap. He ran until he crested a mountain ridge. He paused, standing tall and proud on the ridge and looked out over the valley behind him.

Catamount was tucked into a valley in the foothills of the Appalachian Mountains. Its lights glittered in the darkness. A half moon was rising beyond another mountain ridge. He stretched before leaping forward once again and weaving back down the mountainside into the forest. By the time he reached the yard, he'd only just started to tire. It was fully dark with the stars bright above. He shifted back into human form once he reached the house and quickly tugged on his clothing. A pounding need to see Roxy beat within him. Well acquainted with navigating the thin lines between his human and lion self, he knew shifting into lion form brought him closer to the primal side of himself. Right now, his need to see Roxy went beyond primal and teetered on frantic.

He climbed into his car and drove quickly to town, hoping to find her at the store. He realized he was speeding when he flew past the police station and tapped his brakes to ease up. Coming to a jerking stop across the street from the store, he leapt out and kicked the door shut behind him. The lights were off in the front of the store, but he could see the lights on in the back where the deli was. He circled around the old home and went to the back door. Standing in front of it, his chest tightened. He must've stood here in the darkness a few hundred times that year they were dating. This was where he dropped her off and picked her up. He mentally shook himself. Even though his lion was about ready to pound the door down, he needed to get a hold of himself. Roxanne had made it clear she needed time, and he had to respect that.

He took a slow breath and knocked on the door. After a few moments, he heard footsteps coming down the short hall from the kitchen. The door opened and Roxanne stood there. The light from the hall illuminated her in the darkness from outside. Her eyes widened when she saw him.

"Hey, I couldn't figure out who would be knocking on this door. I should've guessed it was you," she said by way of greeting.

"Yup, it's me. I, uh, needed to see you." His words came out rough. He shackled the urge to step through the door and yank her into his arms.

Her eyes coasted over him. Her hair was in its usual knot, held in place by a pen with a bright pink ball on its end. The frivolous touch made him smile because he knew Roxanne likely hadn't even noticed the small detail. She'd just grabbed the first pen around when she tied her hair up and out of the way. She wore an apron over a fitted blue t-shirt and jeans. Because of Roxanne, he'd always considered aprons sexy. On her, the apron unintentionally accentuated her generous breasts. His body tightened as he looked at her, longing coursing through him. She appeared to be considering something, but then she stepped back and gestured for him to come inside. He followed her into the hall, relieved she hadn't turned him away.

"You're welcome to hang out in the kitchen while I make pastries. I have to get them prepped for tomorrow morning."

Max was happy for any moment Roxanne gave him, so he followed her down the hall into the deli kitchen. She gestured to a stool near a stainless steel table in the center of the kitchen where she was clearly mid-project with flour, bowls of dough and other items scattered around the table. "Have a seat. Want something to drink?"

At her question, he realized he was seriously thirsty, likely due to his hours long run through the mountains in lion form. When he nodded, she pointed to the massive refrigerator on the far wall. "Go see what you can find. Just like before, we have all kinds of juices. I turned off the soda machine though, so you'll have to make do with something else if that's what you wanted."

He strode to the refrigerator and snagged a bottle of cranberry apple juice. As he turned back, a wave of emotion rocked him. This moment was like so many they'd shared before. With a mental shake, he made it to the stool and slid onto it, facing her where she was rolling pastry dough and cutting shapes. He watched her quietly while she added spinach and feta filling to an entire tray of perfectly cut triangles and folded them together. Before she asked, he reached for the tray and carried it over to a refrigerator that held racks for trays. He'd done this for her many times before. When he returned to his seat, she was standing stock still at the table. She glanced over at him, her eyes bright with what he thought were tears.

He started to move around the table, and she waved him away. "No, no." She paused and swiped her sleeve across her face. "This is… I don't know. It's so weird to have you here like this. It's like you were never gone. Except you were and now I don't know what to do."

He again started to move toward her, but she swatted her hand in the air. "No! Don't come over here and hug me because that'll just make it worse."

He had to physically force himself to pause. It hurt to have her push him away, but pushing back wouldn't help. With a deep breath, he eased his hips back onto the stool and watched her carefully, calling upon more restraint than he'd known he had to keep from going to her. She started rolling dough again, this time cutting small circles into it. After several quiet moments, she spoke again. "How do you know this isn't just wishing the past were the present? I mean, even if things hadn't ended the way they did, we don't even know if we'd have stayed together. Maybe we're all stirred up just because of how things ended. How do you know if what you feel is real?" She didn't look up and kept steadily rolling the dough and cutting it into circles.

"Because I just know. It's not like I went away and forgot about you. I *never* stopped missing you. Are you afraid it's not real for you?"

She glanced up and rolled her eyes, eliciting a smile

from him. He'd always loved her tendency to laugh her way through things. "I guess I am, or I wouldn't be asking."

He waited to see if she would say something else before speaking again. "Roxy, all I can go on is how I feel. There isn't even a tiny part of me that doubts how I feel about you. I loved you back then, and I love you now. I get that you need time, and I'll wait."

The rolling pin ceased its rhythmic motion, and she set it aside to carefully place the circles of pastry dough on another tray. "Yeah, but how do you know what will happen? What if you find out I'm not as great as you think? What if…"

He couldn't help himself and cut in. "If I were you, I'd have plenty of doubts. I can't answer all the what-ifs for you, and I don't blame you for them. I left you once. Even if I was young and even if it was a mess because of everything else going on, it happened. All I want is a chance to show you I'm here now and I'm not going anywhere."

She was quiet as she leaned over to place small spoonfuls of a different filling on the pastry circles. A loose lock of hair fell forward and she brushed it away with her wrist. Without thinking, he reached over and tucked it behind her ear. Her breath drew in sharply. She paused in her work for a moment and then continued. He let his hand fall away and took a long swallow of juice.

When she began to pinch the dough together, she spoke again. "See, it's the little things like that. It makes me crazy."

"What makes you crazy?" he asked, drawing on his patience. He wanted to barrel through her resistance, but he knew it might ruin the only chance he had with her.

"It's like you never left. You used to keep me

company all the time like this when I was working here after school and at night." Her eyes brightened again and a tear rolled down her cheek. "You tell me you love me like I'm supposed to just believe it's all gonna be okay. What if something happens and you leave again? I can't deal with it. I feel crazy because this so isn't me. You haven't known me for fifteen years. I'm not a foolish seventeen-year old girl anymore. I've run this place on my own for years. I'm independent as hell, and I never expected to worry about this kind of drama again. It's messy. I don't like it," she declared, dragging her sleeve across her face and leaving a streak of flour on her cheek.

Damn, she was glorious. Even though he should be worried about her resistance, her spirit and will only served to make him want her more. He watched her and tried to gather his thoughts. "Roxy, all I can do is tell you I'm not going anywhere. There's nothing that could make me leave. Even if Wallace were still the unofficial king of Catamount, I wouldn't leave. I'm here, and I'll wait as long as I have to."

She took a deep breath and let it out in an elaborate sigh. "It would help if you felt as crazy as I do inside," she said with a roll of her eyes.

"You think I don't feel crazy?" He stepped off the stool and strode around the table to her. "Not a day has passed when I didn't think about you. I've known for years I blew it and hurt you. It doesn't really matter all the reasons behind it, it was what it was. I'm half out of my mind for you, and I'm doing everything I can not to tackle you every time I see you."

He reached her side and spun her to face him, grabbing her hand and placing it over his throbbing hard cock. "I'm crazy inside and out," he nearly growled. "I want you like I've never wanted anyone and it's way worse than it was before. Trust me, I feel crazy because I can't just throw you over my shoulder and cart you off every time I see you. Intellectually, I get that you need time and I need to let you have it, but it makes me crazy."

He stood there before her, his heart banging against his ribs and his cock so hard it bordered on painful. She hadn't taken her hand away, which only made it worse. Her eyes were wide as she stared back at him. Slowly, the corner of her mouth lifted in a grin. "Okay, so maybe we're in this madness together." She gave a gentle squeeze before pulling her hand away. At that, she returned to her pastry preparations.

Chapter 9

Roxanne leaned over and snagged the bottle of wine sitting in the middle of the table in Phoebe's kitchen. She quickly filled her glass and glanced to Chloe Ashworth who sat beside her. "Need some?"

Chloe held her glass up. "Thank you," she said with a grin, her green eyes crinkling at the corners.

Chloe was married to Dane Ashworth and had quickly blended into their small social circle. With Shana being Dane's sister, Roxanne considered it a lucky plus that Chloe fit in so well. The Ashworth's were another of the founding shifter families. Along with Roxanne's family and the North's, the Peyton's had been the only family of the four that held themselves apart. Roxanne glanced around the table at her friends. Phoebe was busy at the counter. She'd married Jake North and they'd all breathed a sigh of relief because those two had been half in love forever. Jake's sister Lily was seated across the table from Roxanne, busy nibbling on tortilla chips while Shana regaled her with the latest mishap at the hospital, which involved a cat somehow finding its way into the laundry room there.

"Seriously, you should've seen this cat. For four days straight, he kept finding his way inside and napping in the clean laundry. They still don't know how he got in. We finally named him Laundry, and Rosie took him home with her," Shana said with a laugh.

Lily grinned and reached for her wineglass, her eyes immediately glancing around when she noticed her glass was empty.

"Looking for this?" Roxanne said, holding the bottle aloft.

Lily nodded, her golden brown hair swinging about her shoulders. "Definitely."

Roxanne passed the bottle of wine across the table. Conversation carried on around her as her mind spun to thoughts of Max, wondering if perhaps her life might turn out differently than she'd envisioned. In the last few years, all of her closest friends had found love. Chloe had ended up staying in Catamount after hiking her way here on the Appalachian Trail and falling head over heels in love with Dane. Phoebe and Jake had finally admitted they were meant for each other. Lily had stopped playing the shy computer geek and let Noah Jasper sweep her off her feet. Even Shana had moved on from the tragic betrayal and subsequent death of Callen Peyton, her first husband and the shifter who brought the smuggling ring to Catamount. During the investigation of the smuggling network, Shana had bolted to Montana on her own and encountered Hayden Thorne, a powerful shifter from Montana who ultimately followed her back to Catamount.

In the years after Max left, Roxanne had tried dating here and there. Every attempt had been underwhelming. Eventually, she'd decided she was better off simply

enjoying her independence. Her store was a central
gathering place in town, and she was proud of her role in
Catamount—she was carrying on her family's legacy. She
had amazing friends and a fulfilling life. Even while
watching one friend after another find their happily-ever-
after, she hadn't longed for anything like that for herself.
Until Max walked back into town. Damn him. He had a
hold on her like no one ever had. She'd thought she was
over him for once and for all. Her thoughts rolled back to
last night in the deli kitchen when he grabbed her hand and
placed it over his cock. Holy hell. Just thinking about it
sent a wash of heat through her. Her channel clenched and
she shifted her legs, crossing and uncrossing them.

Phoebe turned away from the counter with a platter
of appetizers in her hand. "Coming through," she
commented to the table at large. Lily scooted her chair over
to make room between her and Shana. Phoebe slid the
platter on the table and turned to grab a small stack of
plates on the corner of the counter. "Here we go. Eat up,"
she said with a smile as she slid into the chair between
Shana and Lily.

For a few moments, conversation paused while they
filled their plates with Phoebe's goodies. She was a
phenomenal cook, so whenever it was her turn to host their
dinners, everyone loved it. Their group of friends had
dinners together weekly. Roxanne took a bite of a fluffy
pastry and sighed. After she finished chewing, she looked
over at Phoebe. "Oh my. These are sooo good. What's in
the filling?"

Phoebe grinned, her dark eyes lighting up. "It's an
artichoke filling with cream cheese and tarragon. You
should try it at the store."

"I just might."

While they ate, they chatted casually. They'd all

been relieved after the smuggling network had been shut down because their get-togethers could feature something other than that as a topic. Chloe was regaling them with Dane Jr.'s latest mishap. "I swear, it's a miracle he hasn't broken any bones yet. He tried to climb the banister. Fortunately, he fell off right away, but you know how high that old railing is!"

Shana chuckled. "I think I'm relieved we have a little girl. Sophie's not nearly as wild as he is."

Chloe shrugged. "He's wild, but I love him to pieces. Besides, if you have other kids, you just might end up with your own wild boy."

Roxanne's heart gave a hard thump. She'd let go of any dreams about a family of her own years ago and happily played the favorite auntie to her friends' children. With Max back in Catamount and insisting he loved her, old dreams were rising from the ashes. At thirty-two years old, the wheel of her life was spinning in another direction, and she didn't know what it held in store for her. Someone said her name, knocking her out of her odd reverie.

"Huh?" she asked, her eyes scanning the table.

"Who's Max?" Chloe asked, brushing her honey blonde hair behind her shoulders.

Roxanne almost jumped in her seat. She was that hypersensitive to his name. Chloe was the only friend here who hadn't been in high school with them. The rest knew who Max was and what he'd meant to Roxanne. She flushed and mentally gave herself a shake. *You can't be this ridiculous over him. Max is here to stay, or so he says, and you'd better get used to people asking you about him.* She took a breath and glanced to Chloe.

"He's, uh, an old friend who just moved back to Catamount," she finally replied.

Chloe looked slightly puzzled. "Why's everyone

keep asking me about you and him then? It doesn't sound like a big deal."

Roxanne flushed deeper and glanced around the table. Lily caught her eyes, her blue eyes warm and understanding. Shana appeared preoccupied with the stem on her wineglass, while Phoebe's knowing, dark gaze held Roxanne's. Phoebe had a bold personality and wasn't one to shy away from anything. Her eyes softened as she looked at Roxanne. She glanced to Chloe. "Old friend is one way to describe Max Stone. If you're wondering why people are asking about him and Roxanne, it's because they were madly in love in high school. We all thought they'd be together forever and then Max's mother moved away after his father died. Max broke up with Roxanne and that was that. Now, he's back in town." She glanced back to Roxanne. "Figured I'd save you the trouble of explaining."

Roxanne took a gulp of wine. "No problem. It is what it is." She turned to Chloe. "That's who Max is. I never expected to see him again, so the whole thing's kind of weird."

Chloe nodded slowly. "I didn't mean to bring up a sensitive subject."

Roxanne shrugged. "It's okay. Max is here and says he's here to stay, so I'd better get used to it."

"Is this one of those things where you'd rather not see him?" Chloe asked.

Roxanne almost burst out laughing. She was so desperate to see Max that it was making her mad inside. Ever since he'd left last night, she must've replayed that moment in the kitchen a few hundred times. The feel of his arousal under her palm had been so intoxicating. She wanted him so much it almost physically pained her. She forced her mind off another replay and met Chloe's eyes. "That's the problem. Half of me wishes he'd never showed up here again. The other half wishes he'd never left."

Chloe's eyes widened. "Oh. So it's like that then?"

Roxanne rolled her eyes and took another gulp of wine. "Yup. It's like that then."

Lily caught Roxanne's eyes. "I meant to tell you I ran into Max today."

"Oh yeah? Where?"

"At the police station. I was there to work on their server. It sounds like maybe you're not so sure what you want, but Max is pretty clear about what he wants."

Roxanne's stomach fluttered and her heart clenched. "Good grief, what did he say to you?"

Lily smiled softly. "Well, he was in love with you back in the day, but he was friends with the rest of us too. He said hi and all that, and then he told me he came back because he hoped he'd have a chance with you." She paused, her eyes scanning Roxanne's face. "If you ask me, he's dead serious. I know it was awful after he left, but I hope you don't let that get in your way."

Roxanne almost burst into tears. Leave it to Lily, the reserved, brainy computer programmer, to cut right through to the quick. When she saw the look on Roxanne's face, she leaned over and slipped her arm over Roxanne's shoulders, giving her a quick squeeze. "I didn't mean to upset you."

Roxanne shrugged and gulped in air. "It's okay. Phoebe's already heard me babble over Max. It's all so out of the blue. I just need some time. He's so positive he loves me, but I don't know if it's just old memories or not."

Lily leaned back in her chair and nodded solemnly. Phoebe piped up. "You don't have to rush things, but don't be stupid like I almost was."

"What do you mean?" Roxanne asked.

"You know how I was about Jake. I almost didn't

let myself believe we could work out. I get why you'd be cautious about Max, but don't be stubborn."

Shana grinned. "Roxanne was born stubborn."

Roxanne glared at her. "Hey, I haven't run him out of town yet, so obviously I'm not that bad."

"Exactly. That's why I figure you'll sort it out for yourself," Phoebe said firmly.

***

Hours later, Roxanne walked along the street, the holiday lights in town lighting her way home. She was relieved she hadn't driven to Phoebe's for dinner because she was slightly tipsy from the wine. Chloe had offered to drive her all the way home, but Roxanne wanted some fresh air, so she'd insisted Chloe drop her off at the edge of town. The air was hovering just above freezing. Roxanne wouldn't be surprised if it snowed soon. She turned into one of the paths leading into the town green, walking toward the town's Christmas tree. The lights glittered brightly in the darkness. She reached the tree and came to a stop, lifting her gaze to the sky. She recalled Christmas the year before Max left. He'd gotten her a gift and hidden it under this very tree. She didn't even remember what the gift was, but she remembered him dragging her out here to present it to her. It had been snowing on Christmas Eve. By the time they made it back inside, they were covered in snow and laughing. Her heart squeezed and emotion washed through her. She closed her eyes and took a deep breath of the bracing air.

At the sound of footsteps approaching, she opened her eyes and glanced over her shoulder. As if conjured by her thoughts, Max was walking toward her, his hands tucked in the pockets of his denim jacket. She was becoming accustomed to the effect he had on her. Her pulse rocketed and heat slid through her veins. Her cat nearly purred at the sight of him with his confident stride and the energy he emanated. He stopped in front of her, and her breath caught. "Thought I saw you walking down the street," he said, his voice low.

"Oh. Um, where were you?"

"At the inn just down the street. The house isn't quite ready for me to move in."

"Oh."

You know, your vocabulary is usually a little better than 'oh.' Shut up. She snapped back at her inner critic.

"Do you usually walk around downtown this late?" Max asked, his mouth curling in a smile.

"Not too often. I had dinner with friends and wanted some fresh air."

While her words managed to sound calm and collected, inside she was spinning wildly. Her belly fluttered and need tightened within. Having him close by nearly melted her.

He nodded and angled his head to the side. "Do you remember…?"

She nodded swiftly before he finished his question.

His eyes held hers, tawny gold in the soft glow from the Christmas tree lights. "How did you know what I was about to ask?"

With her heart beating hard and fast, she took a breath. "I don't know. I thought you were going to ask about the time you hid my Christmas present here."

"I was." His words were soft and gruff.

His eyes stayed locked on her. He took a step, coming within inches of her. She could feel the heat of him. She gulped in air, her breasts rising with her breath and brushing against his chest.

Max lifted a hand and traced a finger along her

jawline. She was nearly vibrating with need at the subtle touch. "Max…" His name fell from her lips unbidden.

He closed the tiny gap between them and slid his arm around her waist, pulling her flush against him just as he dipped his head and fit his mouth over hers. The moment his lips touched hers, it was as if she dove into a fire. His tongue swept into her mouth with bold, deep strokes. She met each stroke with her own and arched into him. By the time he pulled away, she was slightly surprised she didn't collapse in a heap.

He looked down at her, his breath heaving. The air around them misted. "I…"

She cut him off. "Come on," she said, gripping one of his hands and turning away. She strode quickly across the green, tugging him with her. He matched her stride until they were almost running across the street. She led him around to the back of the store, fumbling for her keys before she managed to unlock the door. He kicked it shut behind them and spun her around. With her back to the wall, she looked up at him. He leaned his elbows on either side of her head and brushed her hair away from her face.

"You have no idea what you do to me," he whispered roughly.

She stroked a hand between them, curling it over his hard cock and sliding it up and down. "I think maybe I do," she said with a sly smile. Mixed with her intense desire was the old playfulness she used to feel with him.

His laugh came out with a groan. "Okay, maybe you do."

At that, he turned his head and bit her earlobe, sending a burning shiver through her. He moved on from there to trail kisses down her neck. She started tearing at his clothes, shoving his jacket off his shoulders and fumbling with the buttons on his jeans. He stepped back, his lips making their way along her collarbone, and pushed her jacket off. In the dim hallway, their clothes piled up on the floor until he was lifting her against him, her breasts bare against his muscled chest. She moaned his name when he arched his hips against her, the heated length of him pressing against her clit and sending sharp spikes of pleasure through her.

Chapter 10

Max dragged his mouth away from Roxy's neck and lifted his eyes when his name came out in a breathy moan. Her head was thrown back against the wall, her hair a wild tangle around her face. Lust was pounding through him so hard and fast he could hardly bear it. As if she sensed him looking at her, she opened her eyes, her gaze locking with his. She shifted her hips again. He bit back a groan and started to adjust her in his arms. She wiggled free, sliding her back down the wall and shoving his jeans and briefs down around his hips. Before he could think a single thought, she swirled her tongue around the head of his cock and took him in her mouth.

His palm slapped against the wall as he struggled to hold himself upright while she proceeded to drive him mad. She explored the length of him with her tongue and mouth, licking, stroking and sucking, until he thought he would explode. She drew back, her tongue gliding along the underside of his cock, and paused. He managed to drag his eyes open and look down. The sight of her nearly made him come right then and there. Her lips were swollen, her eyes gleaming in the dim light in the hall and her nipples were peaked. He latched onto a thin thread of control and reached for her, tugging her up roughly and yanking her jeans down. She kicked them free as he lifted her against him.

Shoving the silk between her thighs out of the way, he dragged his fingers through her slick folds, groaning in satisfaction at the feel of how ready she was. He reached blindly for his wallet in his pocket, and she arched against him, reaching between them to curl her hand around his cock. "Don't," she rasped. "I'm on the pill."

He froze and looked at her. "Are you...?"

"I'm sure," she answered before he completed his question. "I want to feel you," she whispered, the look in her eyes reaching in and lassoing his heart.

He adjusted her in his arms as she guided him to her channel, slipping her hand out of the way. He held still for a moment, feeling the pulse of her against the tip of his cock. Fifteen years of missing her, and he couldn't have fathomed how intense and right it would feel to be with her again. He stepped closer, inching inside of her as her back came against the wall. Holding her hips firmly with one hand while she curled her legs around his hips, he brushed her hair away from her face as he slowly sheathed himself inside of her. Her eyes started to fall closed.

"Roxy, look at me." His words came out roughly.

Her eyes flickered open again, meeting his. Only then did he start to move, rocking slowly against her. She flexed in his hold, meeting each roll of his hips with her own. Her slick channel throbbed around him, clenching his shaft again and again. Their breath was ragged, and the short hallway filled with pants, groans and whimpers. He felt her begin to tighten and reached between them, swirling his thumb over her clit. Her head slammed back as she cried out, and he finally let go, pouring his release into her.

He held tight as his body slowly eased. Her legs loosened and hung beside his hips. He rested his forehead in the crook of her neck and breathed in her scent. No matter the time or place, she always carried the subtle scent of baking on her—a sugary, cinnamon scent. Her skin was damp against his. She idly stroked his hair, and the lion within him purred its satisfaction. After several long moments, he felt goose bumps form on her skin. The hallway was slightly chilly. He lifted his head and looked at her.

"Maybe we should get somewhere a little warmer," he said.

He wasn't ready to push it, but he prayed she wouldn't untangle herself and send him away just yet. He mentally breathed a sigh of relief when her mouth curled in a small smile.

"Let's," she replied, wiggling against him slightly.

***

Roxanne opened her eyes slowly. The sun wasn't quite up yet, but the bedroom was faintly light. Dawn was breaking, and she needed to get to the kitchen. Early mornings had been a part of her life for so long, she tended to rise easily no matter the hour and how little sleep she'd had the night before. Yet this morning, with her head curled against Max's shoulder and his arm hugging her close to him, she didn't want to get up. She wanted to stay right here and savor every breath. Her palm had landed on his chest during her sleep, and she idly explored the muscled planes. It wasn't that she'd forgotten he had a body to die for, but they'd been young back then. His lanky build had filled out and hardened. He had the body of a shifter—pure muscle and power bundled into a human form.

"Hey there."

At the sound of his gravelly words, she glanced up to find his eyes open. His tawny amber gaze held hers. Her heart clenched and her belly fluttered. "Good morning," she finally managed.

The corner of his mouth hooked in a half grin. "It's most definitely a good morning," he said, his voice stronger. "I suppose you have to get to the kitchen soon."

At her nod, he moved swiftly. "Okay, let me take care of something real quick."

She squeaked as he rose up and slid down her body, his palms tracing the curve of her hips and sliding between her thighs. Searing desire flashed to life inside. He pushed her thighs apart and dragged a finger through her folds. In mere seconds, she was drenched and panting for him. Her hips arched restlessly into his touch as he slid one finger and then another into her channel. Sweet streaks of pleasure raced through her. Any sense of control was lost when he brought his mouth to her, his tongue joining the exploration of his fingers. He traced her folds with his wet touch while his fingers stroked into and out of her channel. Her entire body was humming with need, taut and aching for release. He swirled his tongue around her clit once, and she came in a noisy burst, her cries ricocheting around the room.

With her channel still throbbing, he rose up, his mouth meandering its way up her body. By the time his lips reached her neck, she was frantic again. She curled her legs around his hips and sighed when he slid inside. He seated himself deeply and held still. "Roxy, look at me."

His gruff command brought her eyes open. His gaze burned into her as he started to move. She couldn't look away from the intimacy in his eyes. He moved with slow, deliberate strokes, driving deep again and again and again. From the echoes of her last climax, pleasure tightened in a coil inside until it let loose once more. She tumbled into the pounding release. He drove deep once more, his body went taut and he called out her name before he collapsed against her.

He immediately shifted his weight to her side. They lay still for several long moments, their breath slowing in unison. She finally managed to open her eyes. He was propped on an elbow. "Good morning again," he said with a grin.

She couldn't stop her return smile, her heart light and airy. "I really have to get up now," she said, giving his chest a little push. He moved easily and followed her into the shower.

***

Hours later after Max had spent a good hour helping her in the deli kitchen before she'd sent him away with a fresh cup of coffee, Roxanne stood behind the register barely able to think about much of anything other than Max as she took orders. Conveniently, she'd been doing this for so long, she didn't really need to think to work efficiently. She handed over a customer's change and moved on. "What can I get for you?" she asked as she closed the register drawer.

"A coffee," came the flat reply.

She looked up to find Brad Peyton standing on the other side of the counter. Confusion and a touch of anger rose within. She schooled her expression to neutral. Brad was the only Peyton not in jail anymore. He'd managed to plead out for cooperating with the authorities. She heard he'd been released about a month ago, but she hadn't seen him around town much. Brad's brown eyes met hers, holding a look of resignation tinged with bitterness.

"Just plain coffee?" she asked in return.

Brad nodded, his dark hair falling over his eyes.

"Coming right up," she said, spinning around to snag a paper cup and pour his coffee.

She slid it across the counter to him. Brad handed over a five-dollar bill. When she gave him his change, Brad pocketed it and picked up his coffee. He paused for a moment, as if considering something. She waited, wondering what he might have to say. He finally met her eyes. "Look, I know I don't have much of a chance to make things right, but I'm sorry for what my family did."

His words startled her, and it must've showed on her face. He shrugged and shook his head slowly. "Look, my dad's an ass. Along with Callen and Randall too," he said bitterly. "I'm not gonna act like I'm an angel, but I didn't know how to get out of it once I was caught up in it. I feel like shit about the whole thing. I know my apology might not mean much, but…" His words trailed off. He looked at her resolutely, as if determined not to cower.

She finally nodded slowly, startled at his words, yet contemplating how awful it must be to be him. "I won't pretend what your family did wasn't horrible because it was. You put all shifters in danger because we were at risk of being exposed. I'll give it to you for cooperating with the police because you were the only one." She paused, watching him, and saw nothing but pained regret in his gaze. "Why me?"

"Huh?"

"Why are you apologizing to me?"

"Because I used to love coming here. Even though my family acted like it owned this damn town, you were still nice to me. Seeing as half the town won't even talk to me, I figure I'll make my apologies when and where I can. Thanks for not throwing me out."

Roxanne felt a stab of sympathy for Brad, which she couldn't quite believe. After everything his family had done, it was hard to consider forgiveness. Yet, it was obvious Brad felt badly about what happened. As she stood there watching him, she thought of Max and the suspicions around his father's death.

"I wouldn't throw you out even if you didn't apologize. I serve whoever walks through the door. I have a question for you if you don't mind."

Brad shook his head. "Ask away."

"Know anything about what your dad was up to back when he was managing River Run Mill?"

Brad looked startled and slowly shook his head. "Not really. That's a bit out of the blue. Why do you ask?"

Roxanne didn't want to give anything away about the investigation, so she shrugged. "Just curious. Think about it. I know it was fifteen years ago, but if you have any ideas about that time, stop by and talk to Hank."

Brad eyed her for a long moment. "I'll do that. Don't suppose you'd fill me in on what's behind this?"

She shook her head. "If you want to help out, that'd be great though."

Brad nodded. "Will do. Perhaps I'll visit Hank now. If I can help with anything else my dad mucked up, I'd be happy to. I've known since I was little that he's a power hungry jerk." He paused and took a swallow of coffee. "Anyway, thanks for actually talking to me. I'll be by again soon."

At that, he turned away. Roxanne watched him go, the wheels in her mind turning over her encounter with him. There was enough of a lull for her to take a break, so she asked Becky to keep an eye on the counter and slipped into the back hall.

Max picked up on the first ring. "Hey Roxy, what's up?"

She smiled straight through at the sound of his voice, her hand gripping the phone. "Hey, I only have a minute, but Brad Peyton stopped by."

"Oh, and?"

"Well, first he apologized generally for the massive mess his family created. After we got through that, I asked him if he remembered anything his dad was up to back when he was managing River Run Mill and told him to talk to Hank if he thought of anything."

"Well then. Any ideas from him?"

"Nope, not really, but maybe he just needs some time to think. I figure if he's feeling bad about what his family did, he might be a big help. He's the only one who cooperated with the police when everything went down with the smuggling network, so he's already burned his bridges with his family."

"Alright then. I'm planning to stop by and see Hank this afternoon, so I'll give him a heads up. How's it going?" he asked, shifting gears.

"Same, same. Busy here, but then it's always busy here. How's it going at the house?" He'd told her he was heading up to his family's home to do some cleaning today.

"Pretty good. Honestly, it's not much more than a ton of dust." He paused, and she could hear his intake of breath. "It was nice to wake up with you."

The sound of his gruff words through the phone sent a shiver through her. After he'd left this morning, it had belatedly occurred to her last night was the first night they'd actually slept together. In the throes of their heated, seventeen year-old love, they'd been bound by the limits their parents set. They'd managed to give each other their virginity one night in Max's car when they were supposed to be at the movies. After that, they'd taken every stolen chance they got to twine themselves together. Yet, they'd never fallen asleep in each other's arms and woken up together. Until now. Her heart gave a hard kick, and she closed her eyes at the rush of emotion rolling through her.

"It was," she finally whispered in reply.

They were quiet together on the phone for several beats. She opened her eyes and stared at the wall across from her in the hallway. The hum of voices from the deli reached her, and she gave a mental shake. "I have to go," she said abruptly.

"Right. You're at work. Can I stop by tonight?"

Before she could think about it, she heard herself saying yes. She hung up the phone and stood there. Her heart was pounding and heat suffused her. A sense of joy rose within and suddenly she was afraid. She was forgetting how easy it was to lose herself in Max.

Anxiety bloomed within, coiling tightly around her chest and throat. She forced herself to take a breath. She felt torn in two. Being with Max felt so good—so, so good. Yet, she didn't want to lose the strength and independence she'd gained after she finally got over her youthful, fevered dreams about him. *But you won't. Max loves you. That's what he says, but how do I know he won't leave again? Because now you know why he did. Have faith in him. Just once, let yourself have what you know you can.*

She shook her head sharply, trying to shut up the lobbying thoughts in her mind. Her cat rumbled inside, nudging her to listen to her heart and her instincts. Yet, she had done so once upon a time and it had taken years to piece her heart back together. With Max strolling boldly back into her life, she'd come to learn she'd been fooling herself to think she'd actually gotten over him.

A Catamount Christmas

Chapter 11

Max strode down the hallway at the police station and paused at the door to Hank's office. Hank was seated at his desk, reading something on his computer screen.

"Hey Hank, your receptionist let me in. Hope it's okay I stopped by."

Hank glanced up and swiveled in his chair. "Of course it's okay. Janice buzzed me and said you were here. How are things up at the house? Need any more help with the yard?" he asked as he stood and gestured for Max to join him at the small round table to the side of his desk.

Max sat down and shook his head. "No help needed. Those kids did a bang up job clearing the yard out. It's ready for winter now. Thanks again for organizing that."

"Like I said, not a problem."

"I meant to stop by anyway, but thought I'd pass on that Brad Peyton stopped by Roxanne's Store this morning. She said he apologized for the smuggling fiasco, so she asked him to talk to you if he had any ideas what his dad might've been up to back when he was running River Run Mill. Figured you might want to know about that."

Hank grinned. "Brad already stopped by. I didn't give him any clues as to why we're looking, but I asked him to do some digging into his father's old accounts. He seemed willing enough. When all was said and done, he was the only one who was helpful in our investigation. Maybe it was just to get credit for time served, but my gut feeling was that he felt bad about the whole mess. Wallace was just as much of an ass to his kids as everyone else. Brad was probably afraid of what his dad might do if he hadn't gone along with it when they were running drugs. Way I figure it, Brad can get us close to info we'd otherwise need a warrant for."

Max nodded slowly, a sense of hope he hadn't allowed himself to have unfurling. Given how long ago his father died, he hadn't hoped for much from the investigation, but avenues appeared to be opening. "Alright then. Maybe he can turn something up."

"Here's hoping."

Max leaned back in his chair with a sigh. "It occurred to me that it might not be too helpful to you if I'm stopping by every other day for an update. I'm kind of impatient now that you're actually investigating."

Hank chuckled. "No worries. Stop by whenever you want. Speaking of help though, why don't you dig through whatever records your parents left behind."

"Will do. My mom had a bunch of stuff in storage in Virginia that I shipped up here. I also came across some boxes in the attic today. I'll see what I can find."

Hank's phone rang. He leaned over and snagged it off his desk. Max stood and gave a small wave. "Catch you later."

He headed out for a drive up to the county courthouse. Not much later, he walked back outside after a brief tour of his offices and meeting with the administrative staff. He aimed his car back in the direction of Catamount. As he drove along the winding roads through the mountains, leaves blew across the road. Snow had already capped the mountains nearby, heralding winter's coming arrival. His thoughts went to Roxanne with her all but parked in his body and mind these days. He wanted last night to turn into many nights, yet he sensed a lingering hesitation in her, although she hadn't voiced it aloud.

He glanced at the clock and saw he had a few hours before it was sensible to head over to see her again. Much as he'd have been happy to hang out in the deli kitchen at all hours, like he once did when they were young, he guessed she might not appreciate it. He turned off the main highway into Catamount onto the side road leading to his family home. Moments later, he was carting some of the dusty boxes from the attic out to his car. He'd quickly checked the boxes and was bringing only those with old paperwork in them. Although he'd gotten the house mostly clean, he needed to get the boiler up and running and actually furnish the place before moving in. For now, he'd bring these boxes to the hotel and start making his way through them to see what he might find.

Max stopped to get gas just outside of the downtown area. While he was waiting for the tank to fill, a vaguely familiar man approached him. He guessed the man to be a shifter based on the way he carried himself and the subtle energy he gave off. The man had darkish blonde hair and brown eyes with the distinctive feline cast to his face. The man paused at the front of Max's truck. "Max Stone, right? Heard you were back in town."

Max nodded. "That's right. You seem familiar, but

I'm better with faces than names."

The man stepped closer and rested his elbow on the hood of Max's SUV. "Lee Hogan. You might remember my brother Kirk better. I was a few years ahead of you two in high school."

"Oh right. I had a few classes with Kirk," Max replied. He and Kirk hadn't run in the same circles, although their fathers worked together at River Run Mill. Beyond that, Max didn't remember much about Kirk. Being polite, he asked the obvious. "How's Kirk doing?"

Lee was quiet for a moment, his expression unreadable. "Guess you didn't hear. He was swept up in the arrests around here for the smuggling ring about two years ago. Whole thing was a fuckin' mess. They came down pretty hard on some of the low level guys. Don't get me wrong, Kirk was definitely up to no good, but he was a middle man. He's serving ten years for it, which is ridiculous if you ask me."

Though Max's knowledge about the smuggling network and its eventual fall in Catamount was superficial, Lee's comments didn't sit well with him. Yet, he wasn't interested in letting this topic go any further, so he kept his reply cursory. "Well, sorry to hear about that. How's your family doing?"

"Dad's still alive and kicking. He mentioned he thought you'd moved back to town. How about your mom?"

"She passed away about a year ago," Max offered.

"Oh, sorry to hear that." At Max's nod, Lee continued. "Looks like you might be doing some clean up out at the old house, huh?"

Max was starting to wonder why Lee was so curious about anything to do with Max, seeing as they barely knew each other from before. He again offered a nod, only to have Lee keep going.

"Did you guys leave anything behind when you moved? Hard to believe that place sat empty all these years."

Max was relieved when the gas pump clicked, indicating the tank was full. He busied himself putting the nozzle away and screwing the cap back on his tank. "House was in decent shape. I'm doing a little work to get it ready," he answered generally. "Anyway, good to see you. Give your dad my best."

At that, he snagged his receipt and climbed in his car. Lee stepped out of the way as Max drove away. He couldn't put his finger on it, but something about Lee pinged in his gut. He had nothing other than that to go on when he tapped his dash screen to call Hank.

"Hank here."

"Hey Hank, it's Max. Just throwing this out there, but did Marshall Hogan happen to be around the mill the day of my dad's accident?"

"Yup. He was the manager on duty that day. He and Wallace were the two managers at the mill back then. Why do you ask?"

"No good reason other than a weird gut feeling when Lee Hogan stopped to chat with me at the gas station."

"Hmm. Anything I can work with?"

"Not unless you count my gut feeling. There wasn't much to the conversation, but I barely knew the guy when I lived here before. For what it's worth, he thinks you were too hard on his brother."

Hank chuckled. "Kirk was in pretty deep with the smugglers, no matter what Lee would like to think. Anyway, I'll keep Marshall's role in mind when I'm interviewing the others who were there. The one thing I am worried about is we already know Wallace didn't act alone. I'll need to be cautious when I start talking with the old mill crew to keep word from spreading too fast."

"Right, well, I've got all the file boxes from my parents' house, so I'll start looking through those soon."

"Got it. I'll keep you posted on the rest." At that, the line clicked off. Max angled his truck into a parking spot across the street from Roxanne's Store before he realized he'd done it. For a second, he considered heading back to the inn down the street, but he didn't feel like a quiet afternoon alone with boxes of his parents' papers. He stared across the street at the familiar storefront. Between yesterday and today, Roxanne had obviously set someone to work on holiday decorations. Lights were hung along the windows and someone was decorating a Christmas tree centered in the front windows. He quickly calculated and realized Thanksgiving was a mere week away. In all his planning to move back to Catamount, he hadn't considered the holiday season. He could only hope he'd be welcome at the usual Thanksgiving gathering hosted at the store, although he wasn't sure if Roxanne had kept up the tradition started by her grandparents. He gave himself a mental shake. He didn't need to start thinking too far ahead.

He climbed out of his car and strode across the street. He was about halfway over when Roxanne came out the front door of the store. She didn't notice him as she turned and stood in front of the windows. She wore a pair of jeans with a bright purple shirt that hugged her curves with an apron atop it. Her blonde hair was in its usual knot with a pen sticking up behind her head from where it held the knot in place. As he approached, he heard her talking and realized a window beside the wide center window was open. "Move it a little bit to the left," she said. Whoever was decorating the tree obeyed with the tree inching sideways. "Perfect," Roxanne announced.

She started to turn away and collided with him. Her breath came out in a puff. "Ooh! I didn't see…" Her words trailed off as she glanced up.

He couldn't help but grin at his luck. If only for a second, he got to feel her lush curves against him before she stepped back. "Didn't mean to startle you."

She appeared to be fighting a return smile and finally gave into it. Her eyes sparkled up at him, and it was all he could do not to toss her over his shoulder and carry her away. She took another step back and reached up to adjust the pen holding her hair in place. "I didn't know you'd be stopping by so soon."

He shrugged. "Me neither. Before I realized it, I was parking right there," he said, gesturing over his shoulder to where he was parked across the street. "If you don't mind, I thought I'd get some coffee. If you want help out back, I'm at your service."

She stared up at him for a few beats before answering. "If you want, you could help Joey finish hanging the lights."

"Anything you need," he replied.

She grinned and spun around, walking quickly back into the store. "Joey finished the lights on the downstairs, but we were trying to figure out when I could find someone to help him with the upstairs and roof. Between the extension ladder and managing the lights, it's a two-person job. The rest of us are too short."

Max chuckled as he followed Roxanne through the aisles. Diane threw a grin his way as he passed by, and his heart warmed a little to realize he was starting to feel like he was blending back into Catamount. Roxanne rounded the counter in the deli with him right on her heels. Moments later, they were in the storeroom, the very room where he'd finally gotten his first taste of her after fifteen long years. A young man was standing by the table, carefully untangling massive lengths of holiday lights.

"Joey, I found help for you. Between you and Max, you guys will have this done in no time!"

Joey glanced up, tossing his shaggy brown hair off his forehead. He was all arms and legs, but Max knew at a glance he was related to Hank Anderson. "Max Stone," he said, holding a hand out and stepping in front of Joey.

Joey freed a hand and gave Max a quick shake. "Joey Anderson."

"Okay, I've gotta get back out front," Roxanne said quickly. "You two can sort this out without me, right?"

Joey glanced to her with a grin. "Pretty sure we got this."

Roxanne's eyes flicked to Max. "Thanks for helping out. I'll be out front if you guys need anything."

She spun away and jogged back down the hall. Joey met Max's gaze. "Ever hung lights on a roof before?"

Max nodded. "Sure have. If you're familiar with how much we need, let's get started."

Joey glanced to the cluster of lights in his hands. "They're all right here."

Several hours later, Max stepped off the extension ladder and took a few steps back, his eyes scanning the roofline of the store. "Looks good!" he called up to Joey who was leaning out of one of the attic windows. Joey gave a thumbs up and disappeared from view, closing the window behind him.

Max carefully brought the extension ladder down and carried it around to the back of the building where it was stored inside the massive old barn behind the home. He was washing his hands in the sink by the door when it opened and Roxanne stepped through. She had a streak of flour on her cheek and loose locks of hair fell around her face.

"The lights look great. Thanks for helping out," she offered by way of greeting.

"No problem."

She stood there before him, looking so damn beautiful, he could hardly think. He'd wondered if the heated hum that ran through him at the sight of her would start to ease up, but it only seemed to have grown stronger. Her shoulders rose and fell with a breath, and he fought the urge to yank her to him and kiss her.

"I'm finishing up soon. Becky's handling closing tonight," she said, her words breaking into the silence.

"Do you want to grab dinner somewhere?" he asked quickly.

She was quiet long enough that he worried she was about to say no. She bit her lip and angled her head to the side. "Okay," she finally replied, the word stretching out slowly. She turned away and started to walk back out of the garage.

"So, should I meet you out front?" he asked.

She paused by the door and glanced over her shoulder. "Sure. I just need to ditch this apron and let Becky know I'm leaving."

He took three quick strides to reach her side, dipping his head to catch her lips in a kiss. He didn't know why, but he had to kiss her just then.

Chapter 12

Roxanne climbed into Max's car, still flustered from his kiss a few minutes ago in the garage. She'd tried to persuade herself to say no to dinner, but she couldn't seem to do it. She glanced through the rear window into the back of his car.

"Are those boxes from your move here?" she asked.

He shook his head as he started the SUV and angled it away from the curb. "Nah. Those are from the attic at the house. Hank wants me to dig through any old files I can find and see if my dad had anything saved from back when he thought Wallace was embezzling."

Her stomach churned as she considered Max's matter-of-fact response. If his mother's suspicions were correct, his father had been set up to die, which nearly broke Roxanne's heart. It was bad enough he'd had to adjust to his father dying so suddenly, but to learn it might have been on purpose infuriated her. She glanced at the strong lines of Max's profile. "It makes me so angry that maybe your dad died just because he found out Wallace was embezzling. I swear that man is plain evil."

He rolled to a stop at a corner and glanced her way. "It sucks, but maybe I can find out what really happened. I never stop missing him, but I've had fifteen years to get used to it."

"I know. I hope Hank can find out if your mother was right."

The light changed at the intersection, and Max looked away as he drove through. "Me too."

After a moment, she moved on. "How are things at the house?"

"Moving along. The kids Hank rounded up took care of the mess in the yard, and I've mostly got it cleaned up inside. I need to make a run to Portland to get some furniture before I move in though."

"Can you take me by?" she asked impulsively.

He glanced her way with a nod. "Sure. Let's stop by now. It's not dark yet. Where did you want to get dinner?"

"We might as well go to the Trailhead Café. Aside from my deli, it's the best place in town."

Max chuckled and steered along the winding road out of downtown Catamount. She didn't know why she suddenly wanted to see his old home. She'd driven by it hundreds of times a year since he'd moved away. The house happened to be down the same road where Phoebe lived, so whenever they had dinners together at her place, Roxanne drove by. At first, it hurt every time she saw it, but she eventually became inured to the sharp pang of loss. Over time, the brush and vines had closed in around the house, largely obscuring it from view and her pain along with it.

Within a few minutes, he pulled up at the house. The yard was clear and the home was once again visible from the road. It hadn't changed much, minus the expected wear and tear after fifteen years of Maine winters. She scanned the yard, her eyes searching out the corner where the tree house had been. The two oak trees stood by themselves with no tree house between them.

"It's gone," Max said.

She glanced his way, unsettled by the ease with which he read her mind. "Oh," was all she managed.

"It had mostly fallen down, so we took apart what was left."

"Oh," she said again. *Really, Roxanne? 'Oh' is not the only word you can say.* Her sly side sniped at her insecurity, and she gave herself a mental shake.

"Can we go inside?" she asked, restless to have something to do.

At Max's nod, she climbed out and walked to the front porch. Max followed a bit more slowly. He looked puzzled when she reached for the door handle and it turned easily. "Pretty sure I locked up when I left earlier."

They stepped inside, and Roxanne slowly strolled through the empty rooms, her mind spinning with memories of afternoons here with Max. Max seemed distracted. When they reached the upstairs, he paused in the hall where the folding stairs that led to the attic were open. "What the hell?"

"Max, what's wrong?" she asked as he quickly climbed the stairs into the attic. She followed him up the stairs, her mouth dropping open when she peeked up through the ceiling to find boxes torn apart in the attic.

Max kicked at a broken box. "Dammit! Someone broke in this afternoon after I left. I can't believe this!"

She climbed the rest of the way into the attic. "Why would anyone do that?" She scanned the items scattered about, seeing mostly clothing and kitchen items.

Max shook his head and shrugged, pulling his phone out of his pocket. "I've got a bad feeling someone might know something about how my dad died."

Her gut tightened and a cold wash of fear ran through her.

***

Max stood at Hank's side in the attic as Hank's eyes scanned the area. Roxanne was on Hank's other side, peppering him with questions.

"I mean, why would anyone do this? This house has been sitting here empty for years and *now* someone decides to break in and go through old boxes. What the hell?" she asked.

Hank had been mostly quiet, but he glanced her way and over to Max. "I think Max has a point. Him showing up back in Catamount is rattling somebody. I've just gotten started with my investigation into your dad's accident, but I'm keeping it real quiet. I haven't even interviewed anyone yet. I've been putting together a timeline and confirming who was there. My guess is Max showing up made somebody nervous. After your little convo with Lee Hogan, I'm wondering if your gut feeling was right on. I'd be surprised if this was him though. Too bold and too direct." He paused and shook his head. "Maybe it was though. Lee's always been a pretty impatient guy." He glanced around the attic again. "Any idea if anything's missing?" he asked.

Max shook his head and rolled his eyes. "How the hell would I know? All I've done with the boxes so far is check to see which ones had any old files and paperwork. Those are all in my car. If they took anything out of these, I'd be surprised. Nothing more than old clothes and kitchen stuff."

Hank nodded and pulled his phone out of his pocket. "Let me snap a few pics. I've called two of my guys to come over with a kit to check for fingerprints and get better pics than what I can get here on my phone. I'll wait until they get here before we leave. In the meantime, I'd suggest you find somewhere safe to store those boxes." He quickly pulled up the camera on his phone and aimed it around the attic for photos.

Roxanne piped up. "Why don't you leave the boxes at my store? We have an old safe in the back. There's tons of room in it. It's so solid, it would take a bomb to open."

Hank glanced up. "Good idea. I've seen that safe. It's built into the foundation wall. Your granddad added it when he expanded the kitchen in the back of the house." He caught Max's eyes. "She's right. It would be damn near impossible for someone to get in there. Plus, the store has a security system in place and has people coming and going most of the day."

"You sure you don't mind?" Max asked Roxanne.

"Of course not! Let's head over there now. I don't like the idea of those boxes sitting in your car after this happened," she said with a wave of her hand around the attic.

Hank nodded firmly. "The sooner, the better. No need for you to wait here with me. My guys will be here any minute." As he spoke, the sound of vehicles pulling into the driveway filtered upstairs. "Speaking of..." Hank said as he turned away and climbed down the stairs.

Max gestured for Roxanne to go ahead of him and took a last look around before climbing down. His gut churned with a mix of anger and worry. He didn't like it *at all* that his mere presence in Catamount stirred the ashes of his father's death.

***

Roxanne hefted the last box into the safe and set it alongside the others on the dusty shelves in the back. The safe had shelves lining its walls and a rectangular table in the center. Once upon a time, her grandparents had stored weekly cash deposits in here, along with the store's accounting paperwork and her grandfather's hunting rifles. As her family modernized the store over the decades, deposits were delivered to the bank daily, they made the move to computerized records, and the safe fell out of use. However, its door remained locked and it was as impenetrable as ever. She'd decided only to let Diane know they were storing the boxes from Max's family in here. With the safe always locked, no one would notice otherwise. While she trusted her employees completely, she didn't want some of the younger staff to gossip randomly.

She dusted her hands off and turned around to find Max leaning against the table. His hands were curled on the edge of the table, his shoulders rolled forward and his eyes staring at the floor. A thread of tension ran through his features, which were shadowed in the dim light.

"Well, that's the last box," she said.

He lifted his head, his eyes meeting hers, weariness reflected within them. "Thanks for helping carry them in."

"Of course. You didn't think I'd just stand around while you did all the work, did you?" she asked with a wry grin, attempting to ease the tension emanating from him.

His mouth curled at one corner, his eyes lighting up. "Nah. Not really your style. That's one of the things I always loved about you. You just throw yourself into whatever's at hand."

The ease with which he said he loved her hit her right in the solar plexus—a sharp blow to her very center. Her breath caught, and she felt unsteady for a moment.

She'd become so accustomed to being on her own, to being the strong, independent one that it was strange to have someone care about her like this. Max encircled her in his presence the way he had so long ago—as if she was simply meant to be there. As she stood there staring at him, his gaze grew somber, his tawny amber eyes darkening. Without thinking she took a step, closing the distance between them. He lifted a hand and brushed a loose lock of hair off her forehead, tucking it behind her ear. Her breath became shallow and her pulse lunged.

"I'm sorry about this whole..." she paused, trying to sort out what she meant to say. "...this whole mess with your dad's accident. When you told me about what your mom said, I guess it didn't really sink in. Having someone break into your house like that scares me. It's bad enough you had to lose your father that way."

His hand threaded into her hair with his thumb moving in slow strokes on the side of her neck. She didn't think he realized he was nearly driving her mad. She felt him shrug. "We don't even know if it had anything to do with my dad."

She glanced up at him. "What do you think?"

He closed his eyes for a second before opening them again. "I think it probably did. Let's wait and see what Hank finds out, okay?"

She nodded quickly. Before she thought about what she was doing, she reached up and traced the dark slash of his brows with her fingertip, an effort to wipe the furrow away. The hand in her hair tightened, just barely, before his breath sucked in sharply. "Roxy," he said, his voice taut with a hint of warning.

She suddenly didn't care about trying to keep herself from caring so much, from wanting him with every fiber of her being. Light angled in through the partially open door, catching on his mahogany hair. "Max…" was her whispered reply.

She leaned up on her toes, sighing when she felt the muscled planes of his body against hers. His lips met hers halfway. The heated kisses she'd remembered from years gone by didn't do justice to the way Max kissed now. He was far from the boy she once loved and was now a man whose kisses set her aflame inside and out. His kiss was raw, hot, and possessive. He claimed her mouth with bold strokes of his tongue. She strained against him, savoring the glide of his tongue against hers, the rough scrape of his stubble against her cheek when he tore his lips free.

He tugged at the short row of buttons at the top of her shirt, groaning against her skin when he managed to tug her shirt down far enough that her breasts plumped over. He laved her nipples through her black lace bra while she gripped his head, her fingers sinking into his hair. Her breath came in bursts and soft moans broke free as his hands traveled over her bottom. Arrows of heat shot through her when he slid a hand between her thighs. She was already drenched with need and frantic to have him inside of her. *Now.*

She yanked the fly to his jeans open, sighing when she curled her palm around his cock—hot and hard in the slide of her touch. He moved swiftly and spun her around, his hands moving roughly over the curve of her hips as he yanked her jeans down around her hips. Cool air hit her, a shiver racing over her bare skin. His palm slid up her back under her shirt and down again, the calloused surface sending jolts of heat through her. He kneed her thighs apart, her name coming out in a husky gasp. Her only reply was to arch her spine, pressing her hips back into the cradle of his, a soft moan falling at the feel of his hard shaft against her.

He shoved the thin silk out of the way and stroked his fingers roughly into her folds. She was so wet, all she wanted was to feel him inside of her hard and fast, and she wanted it now. A keening cry fell from her lips as his fingers delved into her.

"Max...now!" she managed to choke out.

He complied in seconds with his fingers sliding out and the head of his cock nudging at her entrance. He dragged it back and forth through her folds, driving her nearly beyond her sanity, until she arched and pressed back toward him. He slid inside in a swift surge, and she almost came right then. He held still, seated all the way inside of her, before he began to move. He rocked slowly against her, the glide and pull of each stroke tightening the pleasure building inside. One of his hands gripped her hip tightly while the other rested at the bottom of her spine, anchoring her into every roll of his hips. Tremors started to ripple through her until she felt like she was hurtling toward a precipice, need driving her. Another deep surge into her channel and she let loose inside, pleasure raying through her in a hot burst. A keening cry echoed in the tiny space.

Max went rigid against her, her name coming out with a guttural groan. He held still for a long moment. Her knees were weak. If she hadn't been gripping the table and had him holding her hip in his strong grip, she'd have fallen. Awareness slowly filtered in. She faintly heard the sound of the hallway to the back opening and closing, the distant hum of voices in the deli reaching her.

He eased his grip on her, giving her hip a soft squeeze before he moved back slowly. She started to turn around, but he pulled her jeans back up over her hips, his practical touch almost a caress. She straightened the rest of her clothes and turned to find him buttoning his jeans. He lifted his head, his eyes slamming into hers. Caught in his gaze, her heart hammered away. Every moment with him, and she fell deeper and deeper into that place she thought she'd left behind. With him, everything felt so right and so easy as long as she didn't think. She stood there, caught in the maelstrom of emotion storming through her. He simply stepped to her and ran a hand through her hair, his palm curling around her nape.

"Were we still going to have dinner?" he asked, his tone light.

Tears pricked at her eyes, and she idly straightened the edge of his denim jacket. She swallowed and took a breath, trying to wrangle her emotions under control. Another breath, and the tightness eased inside. "We should. I'm starving."

"Let's go," he said softly.

They stepped out of the safe, and Roxanne turned to lock it behind them. With his hand gripping hers, she tugged him toward the back door, not quite ready to face anyone else at the moment.

Chapter 13

Roxanne slid a tray into the oven and closed it, quickly tossing the oven mitt on the counter beside her and turning around. "Fifteen minutes, and we'll see how they turn out," she said.

Phoebe sat on a stool by the stainless steel table in the deli kitchen and grinned, lifting her wineglass in a mock toast. "You know they'll be awesome. Everything you make is good."

Roxanne stepped to the table beside her and tugged another stool over. "Most of the time things turn out, but I modified the filling you use and added pine nuts," she said, referring to the small puff pastries Phoebe had made a few weeks ago.

"You modify everything," Phoebe countered with a chuckle.

They were having their weekly dinner at Roxanne's this evening. Chloe and Shana were on the other side of the table, looking at photos of Shana's daughter on her phone, while Lily had stepped to the corner to take a call about a computer server problem at one of the businesses she contracted with. When Roxanne hosted dinners, they usually ate in the deli kitchen, primarily because she cooked so much throughout the day, the actual kitchen in the private quarters upstairs was rarely used.

Roxanne snagged her glass of wine and took a swallow. "What's new at the hospital?" she asked. Phoebe was a nurse at the hospital, along with Shana.

Phoebe shrugged. "Not much. We're never bored, that's for sure. This week was the start of the constant parade of food for the holidays. I swear, every time I turn around there're cookies and fudge everywhere. Speaking of the holidays, are you inviting Max to Thanksgiving dinner here? It's just a few days away."

Roxanne had carried on her family's tradition of hosting a large dinner for locals. Phoebe's question was entirely expected, and Roxanne had already been obsessing about it. If she went with her silly, weak heart, the answer was easy. All she wanted was to be with Max all the time, so of course she'd invite him. Yet, the small part of her heart that she'd boxed away after he left was still occasionally protesting. If she'd learned anything about herself since his return, it was that she'd be devastated anew if things didn't work out with him. That terrified her, so she found herself ruminating over how she could bolster herself and carve out some space inside her heart. Somehow, everything was moving so quickly with him. The level of intimacy had surpassed any memories of what they'd once had, which made her feel restless and edgy if she stopped to think.

Her pause in answering Phoebe was long enough that Phoebe spoke again. "Okay, so you're totally freaking out about this."

Roxanne whipped her head up to find Phoebe's warm brown eyes on her. Roxanne shrugged and sighed. "Maybe so. What should I do?"

"Invite him for the dinner," Phoebe said matter-of-factly.

"That sounds so simple."

"Roxanne, it's obvious Max means as much to you now as he did back then. I totally get why you might be struggling to come to terms with that after the way things ended last time. But, he's made it more than clear he's not going anywhere. Plus, even if you're not sure about the long run with him yet, you'll beat yourself up if you make him have Thanksgiving all alone. He doesn't have any family left here. Back when we were growing up, his family always came here."

Roxanne stared at her for a long moment, pondering Phoebe's words. Part of her was plain annoyed to be getting advice. She didn't appreciate the emotional whirlwind Max had brought into her world and chafed against how vulnerable it made her feel. Yet, her heart had some things to say. Her primal feelings for him ran so deep, it was hard to ignore the rumblings of her cat. She took a slow breath and mentally shook herself. "You're right. I'll definitely beat myself up if I don't invite him for Thanksgiving. I can't even stand the idea of him not being here."

Lily's voice came over her shoulder. "Oh good. I was afraid you weren't going to invite him."

Roxanne glanced over her shoulder to find Lily coming up behind her. Lily hooked her hand on the leg of another stool and pulled it beside Phoebe. She brushed her dark blonde hair off her shoulders and leaned forward to pour a glass of wine.

"You were?" Roxanne asked.

Lily took a sip of her wine and glanced over, her

blue eyes holding a gleam as she nodded. "Uh huh. You're stubborn sometimes. I'm with Phoebe though. No matter what happens in the long run, you'll feel like crap if you don't invite him. Half the town comes here for Thanksgiving."

Roxanne rolled her eyes and grinned. "Fine. I was probably going to invite him anyway, but now it's for sure."

"So how are things with Max anyway?" Lily asked.

Roxanne fiddled with the pen holding her hair in place, one of her nervous habits. "I don't know. Good, really good as long as I don't think. It's just happening so fast. I mean, less than a month ago, I thought I'd never see him again, and now he's here and it's like everything's racing at me."

"I think it only seems fast if you act like you two were never together before. I mean, now you understand what happened. It doesn't change that it sucked for you, but at least it makes sense. Plus, if we were all judged forever on how we handled things when we were seventeen, well, most of us would be screwed," Lily said with a shrug.

"So true," Phoebe added with a grin.

"Give me some time to get used to this whole thing, okay? You two make it sound like it should be simple, but I'm still not sure we've even had enough time to figure out if this is something more than the fumes of our memories."

The oven timer beeped at that moment, and Roxanne spun off her stool to check the pastries. She was relieved at the interruption and more relieved that conversation had moved onto something else when she came back to the table.

***

Max walked down Main Street through the lightly falling snow. It was Thanksgiving Day. The lights he'd helped hang on Roxanne's Country Store glittered brightly through the wispy white morning. After their interlude in the safe, he'd seen Roxanne, but she held herself slightly at a distance. He hadn't managed to spend another night with her. He sensed she was caught in her own doubts about them, and he was fighting himself to keep from pressuring her. The lion inside was nearly roaring its frustration because his feelings for her were so primal and ran so deep. Yet, he knew she was still adjusting to his return to Catamount and his drive to woo her back to the connection that bound them. While she worried he might be running along the tracks of nostalgia and memories, he knew beyond all doubt that what they had in their youth had held strong through absence and distance. He simply had to give her enough space to come to her own conclusions. He was prepared to push the issue, but not until he gave her time first. Roxy didn't do well with pressure. Female shifters were naturally independent and strong, yet Roxy stood above most in those characteristics.

He figured he should be relieved she'd actually invited him to the annual Thanksgiving dinner at the store. It spoke volumes in more ways than one. It most certainly staked out his full return to Catamount within the shifter community and allied the most powerful shifter families at his side. With the undercurrents running through town at his return, that meant a lot to him. While unspoken, he didn't doubt some rumors had started to percolate around Hank's investigation.

Max reached the store and pushed through the door. The retail portion of the store was closed, but even from the front, delicious scents wafted through the space. He walked down the center aisle to the deli area to find a small crowd already. He could hear Roxy's voice in the deli kitchen, but figured he needed to be polite and mingle with the company up front before finding his way to her. He recognized many faces he hadn't yet seen since his return. As he stood there, Hank waved from across the room where he stood by the deli counter. Max walked to his side.

"Hey Hank, figured I'd might find you here."

Hank clapped him on the shoulder. "Glad you made it! I was just telling Gail this morning it would be good to have a Stone family member back at Thanksgiving this year."

Gail was standing a few feet away chatting with someone else, but she paused and glanced over. "Max! We were hoping you'd be here." Her blue eyes were warm as she waved him to her side and pulled him in for a quick hug.

"Good to see you too," he replied as he stepped back.

Gail gestured toward a narrow table behind them. "Go get yourself something to drink. There's a bit of everything."

"Including the best mulled cider you ever had!" Hank added with a grin and a wink in Gail's direction.

Gail smiled. "That's my contribution this year. It's got a bit of a kick though, so go easy."

"I'll have to try it," Max said as he stepped past her to the table.

When he returned, Gail was already absorbed in another conversation. Before he had a chance to look around, Hank nudged his shoulder. "Max, you remember Jake North, right?"

Max glanced to Hank's side, immediately recognizing Jake, his dark blonde hair and blue eyes familiar. Jake carried himself with the unmistakable power of a shifter. Jake had been a few years ahead of Max in school, but their families knew each other. Like Roxanne's,

Jake's family was also one of the founding shifter families, so he held unspoken power in Catamount. Max was gradually piecing together the events that led to the build up and tear down of the shifter smuggling network, and he was aware Jake was one of the central players in breaking the network apart. Max nodded toward him. "Of course I do. Good to see you, Jake," he said, holding a hand out.

Jake shook his hand quickly and firmly, his eyes sharp and assessing. "Heard you were back in Catamount. It's always nice when shifters make their way back home. Sorry to hear your mother passed away."

Max nodded. "Thanks for that. I still miss her," he said simply.

Someone called Jake's name from across the room. He lifted his hand in a wave before turning back to Max and Hank. "I drove by your family's place the other day. Looks like you're getting the house and property back in order."

"Getting there. Hank rounded up some kids to take care of the yard. The house is actually in decent shape, all things considered. The boiler's shot though, so I need to take care of that before I even consider moving in. There's that and the damn break in the other day."

Hank leaned closer, catching Max's eyes. "I mentioned the investigation I've opened into your dad's accident. Jake's offered to do some online sleuthing for me. He'll also keep his ear to the ground about any rumors starting to circulate."

Jake nodded. "Glad to help out however I can."

"What would you look for online? When my dad died, the internet was in its infancy."

"River Run Mill started using electronic records early. I already did some digging today. If your dad's suspicions were right, we'll find the trail. I'll ask Lily to help too. She's a whiz at sniffing out accounting issues."

"What exactly do you do?" Max asked, slightly surprised to learn Jake had already accessed the old mill's records.

Hank laughed. "He's mostly a legal hacker."

Jake chuckled. "That's one way to put it. Technically, I do online forensics for all kinds of things. Most of the time it's legal. If people don't set up security protocols, it's like leaving a house unlocked with a Welcome sign on the door. River Run Mill was ahead of the game in using electronic accounting and records, but they set up their systems well before there were security concerns online. They also closed down before those factors came into play. If you know what to look for, it's easy to access old systems like theirs. I'll do the hunting, and Lily will do the rest."

Max nodded slowly. "Alright then. Sounds like a plan. If you need anything from me, say the word."

"Let me know what you find, if anything, in your father's old papers," Hank said.

"Will do. I plan to take some time to go through them tomorrow."

Jake started to say something else when another familiar figure approached them, Dane Ashworth. Max recalled him as one of Jake's best friends and also from a founding shifter family. In all, three of the four founding shifter families were here today. Only the Peyton family, disgraced and with most of them locked up, was missing from the gathering. Dane immediately held his hand out, his gray-blue eyes catching Max's. "Max Stone, damn good to have you back in Catamount," Dane said with a firm shake.

"Good to be here. Today's like old home day," Max replied with a chuckle. In the weeks he'd been back, he'd slowly encountered old friends and acquaintances day by day, but this gathering pretty much held anyone he'd known well.

Dane stepped back, standing shoulder to shoulder with Jake. They were both tall and lanky with the unmistakable feline cast to their features many shifters had. Max turned and saw a face that surprised him. Noah Jasper stood across the room with his arm about Lily's waist. Noah came from a shifter family best known for constantly causing trouble. Max had known Noah to be quiet and keep to himself, but his father was known mostly for being a heavy drinker and abusive to Noah's mother. In all the years Max had come to Thanksgiving dinners here, he'd never seen anyone from the Jasper family here. As if reading his mind, Dane caught his eyes. "Noah left Catamount not long after you and your mom did. He stayed away while he was in the military. We couldn't have broken up the smuggling network without his help. He's nothing like his dad, or anyone in the Jasper line really. It's safe to say he takes after his mother. Plus, he's married to Lily now, so…" Dane grinned when Jake cast a warning glance in his direction.

At that moment, Roxanne rounded the corner of the deli counter, directing two kids who were walking in front of her carrying platters of food. She wore jeans that hugged her curvy hips and a bright blue shirt with a scoop neck topped with an apron. Her blonde hair was tied up in its usual haphazard knot with loose curls falling around her face. One look at her and lust jolted through him. He'd had this ridiculous idea that once he slaked the fifteen years of pent up need for her, he might be able to get a handle on himself when it came to her. Yet, it was becoming clear it would likely take another fifteen years before he managed that. Having finally had a taste of her again, the burning need for her had only gotten hotter.

"Heads up, you might get run out of town if you break Roxanne's heart," Dane said bluntly.

Knocked out of staring at Roxanne, Max swung to look at Dane. "Huh?"

Jake barked a laugh and shrugged. "Between us, we're married to half of Roxanne's best friends. Both of us have heard about how they'll make life plain miserable for you if you harm a hair on her head. With the way you're looking at her, I'm guessing we don't need to worry about that."

Dane nodded solemnly, a glint of humor in his eyes. "Figured you might want to know where things stand. I told Chloe that Roxanne was more than capable of taking care of herself, but Chloe's pretty damn protective." He sobered and held Max's gaze for a long moment. "Sounds like Jake's right. We don't need to worry."

"Definitely not. I'd have come back to Catamount one way or another, but I've missed Roxanne every day since I left. She was always the woman for me. I'm just trying to be patient and not crowd her."

"You definitely know Roxanne if you know you'd better not crowd her," Jake added with a wry grin.

Momentum seemed to have taken over the room with people starting to meander toward the massive table in the center of the room. All of the small round tables that were usually scattered about the deli had been neatly stacked against the wall and several long tables were pulled together in the middle of the area. Someone paused to greet Max, effectively breaking up his conversation with Jake and Dane. Hank had already been pulled aside by Gail.

Max was considering where to sit when he felt a hand slip into the crook of his elbow. He instantly knew it was Roxanne and glanced down to find her blue eyes looking up at him. Flour was streaked on her cheek, and her lips were rosy. For a moment, everything stopped. The hum of voices faded and there was nothing and no one but them. The air around them shimmered as he stared down at her. His heart gave a hard thump, and his throat tightened. He angled toward her and reached up to trace her jawline with the back of his knuckles. Her breath hitched, and she caught his hand in hers.

Someone called her name, snapping the moment. She glanced over her shoulder. "Just a minute!" She swung back to him. "I didn't know you were here yet. I'm, well, busy in the kitchen, but I wanted to say hi."

"Hi," he said, clearing his throat to get the single syllable out.

She gestured to the table. "Save me a seat by you, okay?"

Her request surprised him. "Okay. Do you need some help?"

She shook her head. "Nope. I've got help coming out my ears with all the kids here. The turkey's on its way out, so grab some seats before we're stuck in the corner."

Her hand slipped from his elbow and she spun away. Max moved, half in a daze, toward the table, uncertain where to sit. Fortunately, Jake lifted a hand and gestured to a pair of seats across from him and Phoebe. Moments later, Max watched while two platters of turkeys were situated on the table. Roxanne came out, tugging her apron over her head and tossing it on the counter behind her. She slipped into the seat beside him.

Chapter 14

Roxanne stood inside the freezer in the back staring at a row of frozen blueberry packages. Maine was famous for its blueberries, and she made a town favorite blueberry pie. She stared so long that she shivered. Snapping out of it, she grabbed a bag of blueberries and made her way back into the kitchen. Ever since Thanksgiving dinner, she'd barely been able to stop thinking about Max. It had been so good, just good, to have him there. She'd promised herself for that day she would let herself enjoy his presence. She'd managed to do just that mostly because Max's presence was like an elixir for her heart, body and soul. Having him there in the center of her world surrounded by family and friends offered a respite from her busy life, and a glimpse of feeling young and carefree again. It also fanned the flames of hope burning inside of her and made her once discarded dreams of a life with Max seem as if they were possible.

As if reality existed to hammer home its point, he'd

knocked her world sideways with another mind-blowing, earth-shattering sexual encounter to cap off the entire day. She couldn't bring herself to tell him he had to return to the inn because she selfishly wanted to fall asleep with him beside her again. The intimacy of waking with him and having him slide inside of her, long, slow, strokes that sent pleasure spinning through her, had nearly undone her. It had certainly been a shock to her system and sent her scurrying to a corner inside of her heart. She was annoyed with herself for being so weak when it came to him and constantly battling the part of her that just wouldn't shut up about how obvious it was they were meant to be. In the days since, she'd come up with one excuse after another about being too busy to spend time with him.

The intimacy was almost frightening in its depth, and it was testing her view of herself. That view didn't include her so easily falling back under Max's spell. And yet, her cat, arguably the strongest part of her, kept growling inside that her fear at facing what lay between her and Max only showed her weakness, rather than her strength. As she wrestled internally, Max stopped by for coffee every day and even tromped into the safe to dig through the file boxes he stored there. The damn safe was now like a glowing neon sign for her because all she could think about every time she saw it was the fact he'd surged inside her in that tiny space with her jeans pulled down around her hips and her desperate for nothing other than the feel of him.

With a mental shake, she walked briskly to the sink and filled a stainless steel bowl with water before placing the bag of frozen blueberries in there. She'd forgotten to take them out to thaw earlier, yet another forgotten task in what was building up to be an impressive list. She wasn't usually forgetful, but she supposed she could blame that on

Max too.

She yanked her apron off and hung it by the door. "Hey Becky, I'm running to the bank while I wait for those blueberries to thaw. Be back in a few."

Becky nodded from the register and turned back to give a customer change. Roxanne slipped into the hall and out the door. A few moments later, she walked into the bank down the street. She knocked the slushy snow off her boots and walked to the back of the line. She should've known it would be busy since it was smack in the middle of lunchtime. She took a step forward when the line moved, glancing back when she sensed someone behind her. An unfamiliar man stood there. He was older with slate gray hair and eyes to match. She guessed him to be a shifter, which surprised her because she knew just about every shifter in town on a passing basis. She mentally shrugged and turned away. He didn't seem friendly, and she wasn't too interested in chatting at the moment. She needed to drop off yesterday's deposit and get back to the deli.

A few minutes later, she strode outside. The weather had been teasing with winter for weeks now. It had snowed lightly during the night, although the day's sun had melted most of it, leaving the sidewalk covered in dirty slush. She stopped at the base of the stairs and looked around, her eyes pausing on the inn where Max was staying. A pang went through her. Every day she kept him at a distance only made her miss him. With a sharp shake of her head, she turned toward the store when she heard her name.

She glanced back to see the man who'd been behind her in line at the bank. "Yes?"

The man reached the bottom of the stairs and paused near her. "Do me a favor. Tell Max Stone to back off."

Her stomach coiled and anger flashed within. Her

cat rumbled underneath her skin. "What do you mean?" she asked, not bothering to keep the anger out of her tone.

"People know Brad Peyton's started looking into his family's accounts, and they know it's all because Max Stone is back and digging up the past. The past is the past and can't be changed now," the man said, his flat gray eyes holding hers.

She sensed he was trying to frighten her, but she was furious instead. She stepped closer and leaned forward. "Max Stone has every right to do whatever the hell he wants. I don't know who the hell you are, but you might want to watch your back. Max isn't in this alone, so be careful who you try to scare off."

She was vibrating with anger as she stood before the man. Though nothing showed in his eyes, she sensed he was surprised at her response. They stood there for several more beats, staring at each other until the man finally turned away. She watched him walk away until he turned a corner down a side street. She yanked her phone out of her pocket and called Hank.

As soon as he picked up, she started talking. "I'm on Main Street and some shifter I've never seen before told me to tell Max to back off. Whoever the hell it is knows Brad is looking into his family's accounts. He just walked onto Valley Street. If you head this way now, you can…"

Hank cut in. "Already in my car. Did you happen to see what he was driving?"

"Nope. He's tall with gray hair and gray eyes. Definitely a shifter."

"Got it. I'm on Valley now. Okay, I see him. Call you back in a bit."

The line clicked dead in her ear. She fought the urge to shift and bolt down the street to follow the man, but she knew now wasn't the time or place. She spun around and started walking briskly back to the store, calling Max as she did. All she got was his voice mail, so she left a hurried message and raced back to work.

***

Max stood beside the smoking pile of ashes in the backyard. He'd spent most of the morning tending two brush pile fires. The years of overgrown weeds and brush in the yard were reduced to ashes now. He carefully dragged a rake through the coals to make sure the coals were cooling before putting the rake away in the garage. His boots crunched through the thin layer of snow on the ground as he walked toward the back porch. He heard sounds in the front of the house and stilled completely for a moment. His car was in the shop for an oil change this morning. He'd hitched a ride out here from Jake who happened to be getting gas at the station when Max dropped his car off. Knowing his car wasn't here to announce his presence to anyone coming by, Max quietly eased back into the trees along the edge of the yard. He heard the front door open and then footsteps in the house. With the home mostly void of furnishings, there was nothing to absorb the sound, so the hardwood floors echoed with every step.

Max inched his way into the trees until he was confident he was completely obscured from view. Then, he shifted into lion form. Fur rippled over his skin and a burst of power raced through him. He wanted the benefit of his lion's much sharper senses and the ability to stay undetected more easily in lion form. He held still for several moments, his senses attenuating to his shift. He easily heard the person pull down the stairs to the attic and climb up. Since he'd cleared out the remaining boxes, there was nothing there to find. He heard a muttered curse and a kick to the wall before a form appeared in the window.

Unfortunately with the angle of the sun, all he could see was a silhouette. It was enough for him to glean the person inside was male. He waited until the man disappeared from view and he heard him descending the stairs again. Moving with stealth and swiftness, he circled through the trees toward the side of the house where he had a clear view of both entrances to the home.

Within moments, a man exited through the back door and walked toward the garage. Max immediately recognized Lee Hogan. He wished he could feel surprise, but he didn't. He fought the urge to bolt out of the woods and tackle Lee, although the need rumbled within. Just as he thought Lee was about to climb in his car and leave, Lee turned toward the trees, his eyes scanning the area. Max was well hidden in the thick of a cluster of trees, which camouflaged his presence. Though Lee appeared to sense something, he shrugged and turned away. After he drove off, Max moved deeper into the trees and took off on a run. With the icy wind blowing through his fur, he let his lion burn through his restlessness with a meandering run through the woods and up a rocky ridge. He paused to look at Catamount's picturesque downtown, his breath coming in heaves and his lion finally easing its urge to dash after Lee and take him down. After a few moments, he stretched and retraced his path.

Not much later after he had shifted back into his human form, he paused inside the kitchen, scanning the area for his phone. When he didn't find it there, he headed back into the yard and discovered he'd left it on the stone wall hours earlier. Jake had offered to come back by to give him a ride back to the shop, but Max was hoping he could use the need for a ride to get a few moments alone with Roxanne. She'd been keeping her distance the last few days, and he hoped to break through the wall she was trying to build between them.

As he glanced down to his phone, he saw she'd left him a message. As soon as he played it, he called her right back. The second she picked up, he started talking. "Are you okay?"

"Of course I'm okay! Why wouldn't I be okay?"

"Because someone is trying to get to me through you. Who the hell approached you at the bank?" he demanded.

"I didn't know who he was at the time, but Hank headed right over as soon as I called and brought him in for questioning. It's Bruce Hogan! Apparently, the Hogan's have family all over the state. He's Lee and Kirk's uncle. Where are you?"

Once he explained, she immediately offered to come get him. "Give me ten minutes. After you get your car, we can stop by to see Hank."

After she hung up, Max called Hank. Even though Roxanne was clearly safe and sound, he was worried she might be downplaying any threats Bruce Hogan made. Anger pulsed through him in waves just thinking about Bruce trying to use Roxanne to get to him. He knew it was likely an effort to throw him off the investigation into his father's death. It was also dead on true that Max cared far more about Roxanne's safety than his own.

"Hank here," came Hank's usual greeting.

"What's up with Bruce Hogan? Roxy called and…"

"I was wondering how long it would take you to call," Hank said calmly. "Before you get too worked up, Bruce is sitting tight in a holding cell. I filed charges for threatening against him. That buys me some time, plus they're totally legit charges. He's flat pissed, but that's his problem, not mine. Don't think he expected Roxanne to call the police so fast. Plain luck I found him before he got to his car. I was already in my car when she called, so I got there in seconds."

"Dammit, I want to make sure Roxy doesn't get caught in the middle of this," Max said, his chest tightening and anger rumbling within. He wanted answers about his dad's accident. He owed it to his parents. Yet, he damn well didn't want his digging into the past to put Roxy in danger.

"Roxanne's fine. She can handle herself better than most. Sounds like she told him off and sent him scurrying," Hank said with a low chuckle.

"Still pisses me off," Max replied, his word coming out sharp.

At that moment, Roxanne's hatchback turned into the driveway. "Hank, Roxy's here to pick me up. We'll be by in a few."

He jogged to her car and climbed in, unaccountably relieved to see her. She started talking immediately as she drove toward the garage. Meanwhile, he simply looked at her. Her hair had fallen loose from its knot and golden blonde locks fell around her shoulders. Her cheeks were rosy from the cold, and she exuded vibrancy and strength. He knew intellectually she'd had nothing more than a passing encounter with Bruce on the street, but she meant so damn much that even a small threat scared and infuriated him. She slowed the car and turned into the garage parking lot. When she came to a stop, she looked over.

"Did you hear anything I just said?" she asked, her tone exasperated.

He looked over at her and shook his head slowly. "Can't say that I did."

"Humph," she said with a roll of her eyes. "What's wrong with you? We're finally getting somewhere on this thing with your dad and you're all zoned out."

He reached across the console between the seats and

tugged her close for a fierce kiss. When he leaned back, she looked startled. "I don't like you getting caught in the middle of this. It scares me, and I'm not about to put you in danger," he said flatly.

She stared at him, opening her mouth as if to speak and then snapping it shut. She flushed and looked out the window. A light snow had started to fall. He could feel the wheels spinning in her mind and sensed her agitation. He'd been doing his damnedest to give her the space she needed, but this was different.

She turned back to him, her eyes dark and fairly snapping with anger. "You didn't put me in the middle of anything. Don't you dare try to go alpha on me and tell me to stay out. You can be worried, just like I'd be worried for you, but that's it. I can handle myself just fine. This is nothing compared to what went down with the smuggling network around here. You forget I can fight just as well as you anyway."

In days gone by, when they'd been growing up together, they'd sparred with each other and friends in the woods in lion form. Females fought with swiftness and grace and could easily hold their own. Roxanne held his gaze with her own fiery one. He knew there wasn't a damn thing he could do about holding her back, but it didn't mean he liked it. Not one bit. He finally nodded, almost forcing himself to do so. "Okay, I get it. Maybe I can't keep you out of it, but at least try to understand how I feel."

"Didn't I just say you could be worried?" she countered, defiantly.

"You did," he replied, a half-hearted chuckle escaping with his words.

She shook her head with a roll of her eyes. "Get your car and let's go meet Hank."

Chapter 15

Max leaned against the wall in Hank's office. Roxanne had just left after a call from the deli because the main baking oven had gone on the fritz. She'd left after throwing a glare between Max and Hank and insisting they stop by the deli later with an update since she had to leave. Hank had covered a lot of ground in the investigation, largely due to Jake and Lily's work.

"Jake can fill you in more thoroughly, but your dad was absolutely right about Wallace embezzling. Between Wallace and Marshall Hogan, those two were a big part of the reason the mill went under. Jake and Lily traced everything, including where the money went. I'm guessing Bruce was on the take, which is why he's rattling cages. It's not like Wallace needed the money, but he was always looking for more. For the Hogan's though, that money took them from scraping by to pretty comfortable," Hank explained.

"So how do we go from this to finding out if they

had anything to do with my dad's accident?" Max asked.

"I'm working on that one. We have a little leverage with Bruce stepping out of line. I'm also hoping Brad Peyton might be able to lean on his dad. Wallace doesn't have much to lose anymore."

Hank's phone rang and he swiped it off the table to answer. While he spoke to whoever was calling, Max leaned his head back and closed his eyes. He wanted to feel relieved to learn his father had been right all those years ago, but all he felt was a fresh wash of grief over the whole ugly mess.

"Hey there." A voice came from the doorway.

Max opened his eyes and rolled his head to the side to find Jake standing in the doorway. "Hey man. Hank was just filling me in on everything you and Lily chased down. Thanks for doing that. Can't tell you how much it means."

Jake shrugged. "No problem. It's what I do. Honestly, it was a pretty easy project, mostly because their system was old and unprotected. Once I found the accounting trail, Lily did the untangling to sort out where the money went. I stopped by Roxanne's for some coffee and she mentioned another Hogan got in her face today, so I figured I'd stop in and see what's up."

Hank hung up and waved Jake into his office. "I was just giving Max the rundown."

"So he says," Jake replied. "What's this I hear from Roxanne? Don't think I've ever met Bruce Hogan."

"He's Marshall's brother. Lives a few towns north of here," Hank said and quickly summarized Roxanne's brief encounter and his subsequent interview with Bruce. "Thanks to your work, he knows we've got the goods on the embezzling, so hopefully he wants to make a deal."

A while later, Max strode into Roxanne's Store and made a beeline for the deli. When he didn't see Roxanne out front, he glanced to Joey who gestured to the back hall. Max headed straight to the back to find Roxanne in the middle of arguing with the propane stove repairman. When she saw Max, she paused for a second and then continued her conversation. After another minute, she'd gotten the propane guy to grudgingly agree they'd waive part of their fee.

Roxanne was nothing if not persistent. Her satisfied smile and quick peck on the beleaguered man's cheek almost sent Max into a fit of laughter. The man left and she swung to Max. "Okay, what'd I miss?"

"Not much."

She cocked her head to the side and narrowed her eyes. "Did Hank go talk to Bruce again?"

"Not while I was there."

Hands on hips, she glared at him. "You should've made him!"

"Look, he said he wanted to let Bruce stew for a bit before he talked to him again. Made sense to me."

"Oh fine! Nothing else then? Just the details from Jake that Hank gave us?"

"That's it." Max paused and took a slow breath. He was trying not to think about it much, but the hard part was coming next. Thanks to Jake and Lily, it hadn't been too difficult to prove his father's old suspicions right. Yet, now they had to see if they could confirm someone had set up the accident that ultimately killed his dad.

Roxanne's hands fell from her hips. "Are you okay?" she asked.

Her question both warmed him and terrified him. She'd always been able to read him easily. He loved knowing they still had that connection. Yet, it wouldn't feel good if he wasn't eventually able to move them past this long phase of 'maybe' they seemed to be playing. She ran hot and cold, and he wasn't quite sure of when it was time to push the issue. He finally shrugged. "I dunno. It's great to actually confirm my dad was right about the embezzling at the mill. I just hope we can confirm who had a hand in his death. I mean, what if it really was a random accident? Accidents happen all the time at paper mills. My dad could have found out about the embezzling and still just had an accident."

Roxanne leaned her hip against the shelving running along the wall. "Maybe so, but that doesn't explain why Wallace called your mother to give his condolences before your dad died. It also doesn't explain why the Hogan's are so determined to keep you from looking into any of this."

"Sure it does. The Hogan's don't want the embezzling scheme brought to light. They made a ton of money off of it. If the authorities can prove it, which they can with what Jake found, they'll be facing plenty of trouble."

She nodded slowly and idly ran her fingertip along the edge of a shelf. "Okay, maybe so, but Wallace's call gives us plenty of reason to suspect it was more than an accident."

"Maybe so." Max mentally shook himself. At the moment, he didn't want to dwell on this. It made him restless and edgy, but then again so did Roxanne.

He took a few steps until he was standing just in front of her. "How about we go grab some dinner at the Trailhead Café?"

She looked up at him, quiet for a long moment before shaking her head slowly. "I need to stay until closing tonight. I'm also behind on baking. Having the oven down even for an hour or two throws everything off."

He bit back the growl of frustration that rose inside.

"How about I help out tonight? I only have this much free time until after Christmas, so you'd better take advantage while you can," he offered with a grin.

She looked away and back at him. "I don't know if that's such a good idea."

Tension knotted in his chest. Her eyes were guarded. He forced himself to take a breath before responding. "Why do you say that?"

Again, her eyes flicked away and back. She shrugged, a sense of uncertainty in her gaze. "I don't know. Max, this is all happening so fast. I never thought I'd see you again and here you are. I want…" She paused and shook her head sharply. "I don't know what I want. I just want time to make sure. It feels out of control. I know you say you're sure about how you feel, but I…I feel like it's too soon to tell. We're in a honeymoon phase, or something like that. Just give me some time to figure things out. When you're around, well, I can't think straight," she said bluntly.

He absorbed her words and wanted to grab her and drag her away to show her with his hands and his body just how strong the bond between them was. It was a living, breathing force that couldn't be denied. He forced himself to take another breath, again trying to slow down before he got too demanding with her. In their youthful love, they'd rarely argued, but when they had, Roxanne's passionate nature showed itself in her anger. He knew if he tried to push her, she'd likely push back. Hard. Another breath and he met her eyes again. He'd be damned if he'd be anything but plain honest with her. "I know it's happening fast, but not for me. I've waited fifteen damn years to make right what we lost once. What we had back then, we still have today. I know it with every part of me. I'll try to be patient, but you have to know I don't have any doubts about us and never will."

Her eyes glistened with tears, and she took a shaky breath. "Okay. Just give me a little space."

"I'll try, but it's a kinda confusing to have you say this while you're also putting yourself right in the middle of the investigation into my dad's accident." He hadn't considered his words when they came out, but he was confused and hurt. She seemed to want to call the shots on when she was involved and when she wasn't.

She looked taken aback. "Max, I'm just trying to help."

"I know, but you have to admit you're sending some mixed messages. You want me to keep my distance and give you space, yet you're also sticking your nose right into the middle of something really important to me. It's confusing. That's all I'm saying."

At that, he willed himself to take a step back. His lion was rumbling inside. Having Roxy close by elicited his primal side, and he needed to keep it on a leash for now. He turned away. "I'll get out of your hair. I know you've got work to do." He didn't give her a chance to reply and spun away, nearly stalking down the hall on his way out.

***

Roxanne kicked the snow off her boots as she stepped into the back hall at the store. With the wind howling and snow falling heavily, Catamount was in the midst of its first winter storm of the season with Christmas a mere week away. She closed the door behind her and quickly removed her jacket, shaking the snow off before she hung it on the row of hooks by the door. It was near closing time for the deli, and she was returning from a day trip to Boston to stock up on baking and cooking supplies before the last burst of the holiday rush next week.

She slipped on a pair of clogs and stood there for a

long moment. She was feeling lonely and out of sorts and had been ever since she'd asked Max to give her some space. In the intervening week, he'd kept his distance, and she hated it. She leaned against the wall and sighed, fighting against the tears welling. She hadn't meant to make it seem like she was playing games, but looking back, she could see how she sent mixed messages. She'd been so overwhelmed with her feelings, she couldn't turn away from the passion that snapped and crackled between them. Then, she tried to pull back. At first, she felt like she'd been the one who was hurt, the one who deserved to have amends made. Yet, now that she more fully understood the circumstances around how Max's father died and his mother's fears about keeping him away from Catamount, she could only dole out so much blame to Max.

Ever since she'd drawn that clear line with him, her heart ached as much as it had those years ago after Max left. Even worse, she knew he was nearby and was only steering clear because she'd asked him to do so. The door opened at the end of the hall and Diane stepped through, striding quickly toward the storage room where they kept stock for the grocery section. Diane glanced up, her eyes widening when she saw Roxanne.

"Hey you! Been wondering when you'd be back. How was the Boston run?" Diane asked.

Roxanne pushed off of the wall and tried to summon a smile, but it wobbled. Diane had stopped by the doorway into the storage room and started walking again, pausing when she reached Roxanne. "Hey," she said softly. "Are you okay?"

Roxanne started to nod and then promptly burst into tears. Diane pulled her in for a hug, stepping back and giving Roxanne's hands a squeeze. "Did something happen in Boston?"

Roxanne sniffled loudly and dragged her sleeve across her face. "No. I got everything we need. I was just coming in to ask Joey to help unload everything. I needed a few minutes before heading back out because the drive back was a little hairy with the snow."

"Okay. I've never seen you cry over bad roads though," Diane said with a puzzled look in her eyes. "What gives?"

Roxanne took a breath. "This whole thing with Max has got me feeling all crazy. I don't know what to do, and I'm afraid I messed up."

Diane leaned against the wall across from her and angled her head to the side. "Ah, I see. I thought you said you wanted some space. Max has been scarce around here since last week, so it seems like he's doing what you asked."

Emotion tightened Roxanne's throat again when she nodded. Of course, Max had to go and do precisely as she requested, reminding her yet again that he was a good man who respected her. "He is."

Diane watched her for a moment, her eyes narrowing. "So what's the problem then?"

"I guess I don't really want that much space," Roxanne finally replied.

Diane smiled slowly. "Well, good on you for figuring that one out. Why don't you clue him in then?"

Roxanne sighed. "Because I feel like an idiot and I don't want it to seem like I'm playing games. I guess I wanted time for things to move slowly more than I wanted space."

"I'm thinking you need to let him know this, not me," Diane said pointedly.

Roxanne rolled her eyes. "I know that. I'm just all out of whack. I still can't believe he's here."

"That he is. Look, whatever you do, don't let your pride get in the way."

"Are you saying that's what I'm doing?"

Diane shook her head. "No, just that I know you might have a tendency to be stubborn," she said with a soft laugh.

Roxanne took a breath, the tightness in her chest easing with Diane's playful observation. "Fair enough. Well, you've got plenty to do other than give me a pep talk. I'll go get Joey and…"

Diane cut in as she pushed away from the wall. "You go grab him. I'll help him unload if you can cover the front for a little bit. If you don't mind getting it, I was coming to get a box of cranberry jelly to fill the display up front."

"Deal!"

Roxanne strode swiftly to the storage room. With the box of cranberry jelly in her arms, she headed out front to fetch Joey, while Diane started putting her jacket and boots on to unload the store truck.

Chapter 16

Hours later, Roxanne turned the sign in the front window to closed and locked the door. She'd sent everyone home early and practically shoved Diane out the door. The snowstorm had gotten worse as the evening wore on. Snow was blowing sideways and falling so heavily, Main Street was now completely obscured. She walked through the quiet store with nothing but the sound of the snow blowing outside. Entering the deli kitchen, she scanned the room to make sure everything was turned off. She wished Max were here. She'd love nothing more than to curl up beside him upstairs and wait out the snowstorm in front of a fire. The wish to see him was so powerful, she physically ached inside. She recalled Diane's comment about her pride and shook her head. She'd gather the nerve to talk to Max soon —one way or another.

She headed down the back hall to the entrance that led upstairs and jumped when the door to the back parking lot flew open. The lighting in the hall was bright, so she clearly recognized Lee Hogan. Before she could speak, he grabbed her arm and yanked her roughly outside. She fought against his hold, her instincts taking over. She started to shift, feeling the power rumbling through her body.

"Oh no you don't," Lee said.

She felt a prick in her shoulder and was suddenly weak. Lee dragged her to his truck and shoved her inside. She maintained enough awareness to know he'd just drugged her, but her thinking was foggy and she felt like she was swimming underwater with everything muted and blurred. She tried to rally inside, but she couldn't seem to fight against whatever he'd injected into her arm. He gunned his truck and spun out onto Main Street. Determined to know where he was taking her, she managed to keep her eyes open, but just barely. To her surprise, he took her straight to his father's home. His mother had passed away from cancer a few years back, so as far as she knew only his father lived here. When he brought the truck to a jerking stop, he looked over at her.

"Should've given you a bit more. Doesn't matter though. You're just leverage," he said, slamming out of the truck and coming around to her side.

She was shivering in the cold since she obviously hadn't managed to get a jacket on after he grabbed her. When he dragged her out of the truck, the icy snow pelted against her cheeks and a forceful shiver raced through her. Lee kept a hand clamped on her arm as he tugged her into the house. She'd never been in the home and only knew it because the Hogan's were shifters. It was a small ranch home, fairly nondescript on the outside with gray siding. He brought her through a side door into the kitchen where he thrust her into a chair. The kitchen was empty.

She looked around groggily, taking in the counter

running along one wall with the stove and refrigerator on another. She was seated at a round table with chairs. The walls were dingy white, and the room was void of any decorative touches. Lee strode away, not bothering to say anything else. She heard his footsteps along a hall visible through a doorway and then a mumble of voices. After a few minutes, Lee returned with his father following more slowly. Lee looked quite a bit like his father. They shared the same flat brown eyes and dull brown hair, but Marshall Hogan now had streaks of gray in his hair. He sat across the table from Roxanne and eyed her.

"Roxanne Morgan," he said slowly.

She looked over at him, annoyed with how slow everything felt inside, yet also wrestling against an underlying fear. The drug had clearly affected her strength, but she was still herself mentally, albeit in a muddied sense. Annoyance flared, but she stayed quiet.

"Well, you got yourself caught up in the wrong mess this time," Marshall said. "You and your friends were all high and mighty after you got all those shifters locked up. I don't give a damn about the smuggling network, but one of my boys is behind bars because of it. I won't let Max Stone and your friends make trouble for me now. I won't bother lying. I did Wallace's dirty work at the mill, and we embezzled a shit ton of money. Mill went under and that was that. I had nothing to do with Max's daddy's death, but I'm not going to join my boy in jail over this mess. Lee figures you're Max's soft spot, so we'll keep you here until we can negotiate with ol' Hank Anderson."

Roxanne absorbed his words, trying to clear the fog in her brain. She didn't know if she was on target because she was half out of it, but she believed Marshall when he said he didn't have anything to do with the accident that killed Max's father. But it didn't change the reality that she was drugged and trapped at their house. No one knew where she was and likely wouldn't even notice until tomorrow morning when she didn't show up in the deli kitchen for work.

***

Max heard a loud knock on the door to his room at the inn. He'd just finished showering and dressing. When he opened the door, Hank stood there.

"Roxanne here?" Hank asked, not bothering to say hello.

"Uh, no," he replied, concern rising swiftly inside.

Hank's eyes widened slightly. "Dammit. I was hoping she was here. When's the last time you heard from her?"

"It's been almost a week."

Hank nodded sharply. "Come on then. She didn't show up for work this morning. Diane already checked upstairs at the store, and it doesn't even look like she slept there last night. I figured she must be with you, but now it looks like no one knows where she is."

Max's gut clenched. He spun away, grabbed his jacket and stuffed his feet in his boots. "Let's go."

He jogged down the steps behind Hank and climbed into his patrol car. "Anyone have any ideas where she might be?"

Hank shook his head and backed up swiftly. "Nope. I gotta say, when Diane called, I told myself it was probably a simple answer—she was with you. But I had a bad feeling and now it's way worse."

Hank sped to the police station. In short order, he'd called in supports to fan out across Catamount and look for Roxanne. Her car was right where it should be, but the back door to the store had been left unlocked. If anyone had been there, the heavy snow had obscured tire and foot tracks. Max was barely able to contain himself as he paced back and forth in Hank's office.

Hank took a call and became still and quiet. Considering the last hour had been a rapid-fire series of calls and chatter, Hank's stillness was odd. Max turned toward him.

"Okay Marshall. If you want to talk, I'm more than happy to listen," he said slowly. "Should I plan to come out to your place?"

Hank paused, listening intently. Max stepped to his side, and Hank held a finger up. "Marshall, I understand you're concerned about the situation, but keeping Roxanne there isn't going to help anyone, least of all you."

Max spun away, ignoring Hank when he tried to grab his arm. As soon as he got outside, he started running. He fought the urge to shift because shifting in plain sight was dangerous, but he ran as quickly as he could. He knew Marshall's house was only blocks away and made it there within a few minutes. As he turned down the drive, he heard a car behind him and glanced over his shoulder to see Hank's patrol car. Hank rolled the window down.

"Max, wait up. Marshall's willing to talk, so let's let this play out," Hank said.

"Not unless he releases Roxanne immediately," Max said, anger rolling through him in waves. He could barely allow himself to consider his underlying fear for her, so he let the anger pour through him. It was the only thing keeping him together.

Hank turned into the drive and climbed out. He stood shoulder to shoulder with Max. Though Max knew Hank had enough sense not to shift in broad daylight, he emanated strength and power. Max knew if he tried to shove Hank out of the way, he'd have a fight on his hands.

He clenched his fists and took a slow breath, letting it out in a hiss.

"What's the damn plan? It better not involve letting them use Roxanne for leverage."

Hank watched him for a moment before replying. "Bit late for that. They already have her. Marshall let me talk to her. If you'd waited around, you'd have been able to talk to her yourself. She sounds a little out of it, but she's alive and said she's not hurt. I'm guessing Lee drugged her. Don't see how else he'd have been able to take her. She'd have shifted, and she's a helluva a fighter."

Another bolt of anger shot through Max, and he started to stride toward the house again. Hank clamped a hand on his arm and held firm. Max shook free and kept moving. Hank followed at his side, talking rapidly. "Fine, if I can't talk you out of it, let's not make it worse. You might put Roxanne in more danger than she already is by going in blazing. Marshall wants to talk, so let's let him."

Hank's words sank in through the haze of anger, and although Max couldn't bring himself to agree out loud, he kept himself from shifting and stopped when they reached the door. "Plan?" he asked abruptly.

Hank spoke under his breath. "I've got back up through the trees behind the house and down the street. I do the talking. You wait outside unless Marshall agrees you can come in. Got it."

Max nodded, figuring he could circle the house outside and hone in on where Roxy was. At Hank's knock, the door opened and Lee stood there. His eyes flicked between Hank and Max. "Just you," he said, pointing to Max. He swung to Max, smirking slightly. "You'll have to wait."

As soon as Hank crossed the threshold, Lee slammed the door shut. Max shackled the urge to shift and leaned against the railing on the small porch. He'd give it a few minutes before circling the house.

***

Roxanne had been escorted to a small bedroom at the end of the hallway at some point during the night. She could hear voices, but couldn't make out anything that was said. The room contained a single bed pushed against the wall and a small table. The sole window was too tiny for her to climb through. The night had moved slowly. She'd vacillated in and out of consciousness at points even though she fought against it. The sedative they'd given her made it nearly impossible to stay awake at times. This morning though, she was partially relieved she'd slept a bit because she felt stronger. She still wasn't one hundred percent, but she thought she could successfully shift now. The only reason she hadn't yet was she was biding her time and waiting for the best moment.

She stepped quietly to the door, straining to listen. She thought she recognized the sound of Hank's voice, but she couldn't be sure. She didn't think Marshall and Lee intended to hurt her, yet their backs were against the wall and they'd created a dangerous situation. She didn't doubt they'd do what they needed to take care of themselves. Max had been in her thoughts all night long. All she wanted was the chance to make sure he knew how she felt. Her reasons for needing some time and space hadn't been entirely irrational, but now they paled in the face of realizing she might miss the chance to make sure he knew her true feelings. She'd never stopped loving him and never would.

Hot tears pricked at the back of her eyes. Her emotions were raw. Aside from everything else, the sedative had weakened her emotional defenses and every emotion inside was just under the surface. She wondered where Max was now and if he knew anything about where she was. The mumbling voices were useless to her, so she slowly circled the room, scanning for options to get out. If she shifted, she'd have the strength to break the window out altogether. It was one of those narrow, crank-type windows that only opened on the lower half. If she broke through it, she could get outside into the forest and bolt. Problem was, she wanted to be here to help if something else happened. Given Marshall's comments last night, she guessed he intended to contact Hank and try to negotiate options for himself using her as leverage.

Her mind wheeled onto the remaining question of who had a hand in the accident that killed Max's father. If it wasn't Marshall, then that left Wallace. As she pondered, she heard a sound outside and moved to the window to see Max making his way slowly through the trees behind the house. Her heart jump-started with a mix of joy and fear. She was overjoyed he was here to find her and afraid of what might happen if he tried to intervene. She could stand getting hurt herself, but she didn't want him hurt.

Just as these thoughts were passing through, she saw motion out of the corner of her eye. Lee had shifted and dashed through the yard toward Max. Max shifted in a flash. She didn't even think and shifted, immediately leaping at the window. Her first effort broke through the lower portion. Backing off, she circled the room and barreled forward to the window again, this time the frame gave way and she bolted outside, glass and debris falling around her. Lee hadn't caught up to Max yet. Max was weaving through the trees and leaping off of branches as he took Lee on a merry chase through the woods.

Intense power surged through her, along with primal anger. She ran straight for Lee and swiped at his haunches, knocking him to the ground. He hadn't heard her approach, so she had surprise on her side. She dimly heard Max's roar from a tree nearby, but she ignored him. She went after Lee, attacking fiercely. She got several strong swipes in and drew blood along his front shoulder, but he rolled and managed to leap to his feet. She took chase as he tried to dodge her again and again. He was a bigger, heavier cat. Her smaller size and quicker agility kept him from shaking her free. She felt Max come alongside her. He snarled and tried to shoulder her out of the way. She dodged him and increased her speed, darting ahead to spin Lee to the ground again with a vicious swipe at his hind legs.

He fell to the ground, and she pounced, pinning him by the throat before he had a chance to get up. Max snarled and again tried to shoulder her out of the way. She snarled right back. This was her fight. Lee fought against her hold for a moment, but eventually gave up. She hadn't realized Hank and Marshall had come out of the home, only glancing up when she heard Hank say her name. He remained in human form, as did Marshall. When he approached, Lee shifted back into human form, dirty and blood-streaked.

Chapter 17

Max stood in the forest, his breath heaving and primal anger and desire warring inside of him. Roxy stood nearby, her side streaked with blood. He'd seen her burst through the window and run straight for Lee, and he'd raced in her direction, an intense protectiveness driving him. He should've known she wouldn't care much for his interference because she snarled right back at him when he tried to push her out of the way. He'd forgotten how glorious she was in lion form—tawny grace and strength and feisty as hell.

In short order, Hank had cuffed Lee and Marshall. His two back ups had arrived on scene sometime during Roxy's takedown of Lee. What little leverage Marshall and Lee had gained by kidnapping Roxy had been completely lost, and they'd only set themselves up to face more charges. Max's lingering question was whether or not he'd ever find out who was behind his father's deadly accident at the mill. Right now though, all he wanted was to make sure Roxy was okay.

Over the bustle of Hank and his deputies dealing with the arrests, Max and Roxanne shifted back into human form and dressed in their torn clothing. When Max approached her, her eyes locked with his and it felt as if the connection between them was alive, so powerful it was almost visible in its electricity.

He reached her side and lifted his hand, carefully tracing along one of the scratches on her neck. "You okay?" he asked, fighting against the urge to yank her into his arms and drag her away somewhere private.

She nodded. "Most of the scratches are from when I broke through the window." Her eyes held his for a long moment before she spoke again. "Are you okay?"

"Not a scratch."

The space between them felt crowded with emotions. She was quiet again for a few beats. "With all that, I don't even know if Hank found out anything new."

"Me neither." He glanced around and saw Hank talking with one of his deputies. He caught Hank's eye and called out. "Do you want us to wait here, or would it be better if we met you back at the station?"

Hank said something to the deputy and strode over to them. "Catch us at the station in a little bit. We've got plenty to handle here for now that you can't really help with." His eyes flicked to Roxanne. "You feeling okay?"

"Just fine," she replied quickly.

"Maybe you want to swing by the hospital for a quick check. I'm not so worried about the scratches you have, but do you even know what they drugged you with?"

Roxanne rolled her eyes. "Some kind of sedative. I don't think it's necessary to get checked out. I'll…"

Max cut in. "I'll take you. Hank's right. Who knows what it was? Let's just get a quick check."

She looked between them and sighed. "Fine. It's not worth fighting about. Hopefully Phoebe or Shana's on duty, so they'll make it quick."

***

Roxanne climbed out of Max's SUV behind the store and glanced up at the sky. It was still early afternoon. The sun was bright against the blue sky. Last night's snowstorm had dumped over a foot of snow on Catamount, and the sun struck sparks off the melting drops on the trees. It was hard to believe only hours ago she'd been locked in that tiny bedroom at the Hogan's. She started to approach the back door when she recalled she didn't have her keys. What with Lee dragging her out in the darkness, she didn't have anything with her. Max had insisted she wear his lined denim jacket. She savored the feeling of his scent surrounding her as they walked through the snow around to the front of the store.

When they stepped inside, Diane rounded the check out counter and enveloped her in a hug. Stepping back, her eyes coasted over Roxanne. "You have no idea how relieved I am to see you! I knew something was wrong when you weren't upstairs this morning and the back door was unlocked." Her eyes bounced between Roxanne and Max. "Thanks for calling me once you were on the way to the hospital," she said to Max.

"No problem. I figured you might be worried," he replied.

A customer approached the counter, and Diane stepped away. "Go get some rest. Becky called in reinforcements, so they don't need you in the deli at all today."

As they walked through the aisles and to the back hall, Max's hand rested on her low back, the heat like a brand on her. The long, strange night and the flash of fear for his safety this morning when she saw Lee bolt toward Max had left Roxanne feeling raw. For so long, she'd prided herself on having a handle on her emotions. After she'd picked up the pieces after Max left, she'd honed her strength and control, relying on the qualities that kept her heart safe and sound behind walls. Now, that control had utterly deserted her. All she wanted was to find release for her pent up emotions, which were spinning wildly inside of her.

Neither of them spoke as they walked down the hall and up the stairs. When they stepped into the kitchen, she walked through to the living room and immediately knelt to start a fire in the polished granite fireplace. She didn't know why, but she needed the warmth and comfort of a fire. Within moments, a fire was taking hold and she stood, turning to find Max just beside her with his elbow resting on the mantle. Sunlight fell in a slant through the tall windows, gilding his mahogany hair. His gaze caught hers, and she couldn't look away.

He angled his head to the side. "How've I been doing on giving you space?" he asked.

Her throat tightened as she nodded. "You've been doing great. Too great, really." A wash of fear rose within her, and she batted it away. She loved him. She had always loved him and either she allowed her fear to hold her back, or she let herself trust in what lay between them. She took a step closer and lifted her hand, bringing it to rest on his chest where she could feel his heart beating. "I didn't mean to push you away," she said, her voice cracking.

His eyes never broke from hers. He took a step closer and threaded his hand into her hair, cupping the side of her neck. "I did the same thing once upon a time. It took me fifteen years to make it back to you, so I figured if you needed some space, it was the least I could do. You're it for me, so I need to know you're here on your own terms, not mine."

A tear rolled down her cheek. He brushed it away with his knuckle. She swallowed, barely able to contain the depth of emotion rising within her. "I'm here. I'm still scared, but if there's one thing I learned this last week, it's that knowing you're near and not being with you makes me crazy. I missed you so much, and you were right here." A sob escaped and he pulled her close, his embrace warm and strong and everything she needed. After a few moments, the taut emotion inside morphed into a desire. His hard, muscled body against hers was like a drug.

She leaned her head back to look up at him. His eyes canted down, heat and pure needed reflecting back at her. She lifted a hand and traced his lips. His breath came out in a hiss and his mouth crashed against hers. In seconds, she felt like she was on fire inside and out. A mere week without his touch and she was desperate. Clothes were yanked off in a rush between hot, drugging kisses. Roxanne found herself standing in front of Max where he was seated on the couch. The fire snapped and crackled behind her, chasing the chill out of the room and matching the heat between them.

His hands coasted down her sides, caressing the curve of her hips. Impatient, she stepped closer and rested a knee on the couch beside him. His arousal was blatant—his cock ready and waiting for her. All she wanted was to feel him inside of her. He slipped a hand between her thighs just as his mouth closed over a nipple. He bit down right when he stroked two fingers into her channel. She cried out, the subtle sting of his bite a balm to the need clawing inside of her. She was so wet she could hardly bear it. With his fingers sliding back and forth, she straddled him and shoved his hand out of the way. Curling her palm around his velvet length, she rose up and positioned him at her entrance. Another soft bite on her other nipple, and she lost focus, crying out. He pulled his mouth away.

"Roxy, look at me."

When she dragged her eyes open, he tangled his hand in her hair and slowly shifted his hips. His other hand gripped her hip and eased her down onto him inch by inch. Held in his dark gaze, she trembled. With a subtle thrust, he filled her completely. They were still for several breaths, the air around them shimmering with desire. He slowly began to move, and she rolled her hips in tune with his. In a slow dance, held fast in his gaze, she tumbled into the incandescent connection between them. Every stroke brought her closer and closer to the edge. Pleasure coiled tighter and tighter inside until he stroked his thumb right where they joined. She flew apart, crying his name. A deep surge within, and he flew with her, his head falling back with a guttural cry.

She slowly drifted down, resting in his strong embrace. His hand eased in her hair and he idly sifted through it. She eventually opened her eyes. His head was resting against the back of the couch. He must've sensed her gaze and opened his eyes.

"Hey there," he said softly.

A giggle burst out. "Hey."

He smiled and then sobered. "I love you," he said, the words grabbing her heart.

She blinked back tears. "I love you too. I'm so glad you're home again." She leaned forward and tucked her head into his shoulder, savoring his very presence.

Epilogue

Max opened his eyes and took a deep breath, savoring the feel of Roxy's lush body curled up against him. It had been a busy week since Lee and Marshall had kidnapped Roxy in a failed attempt to use her as leverage to negotiate with the police. Every single night that had passed since then Roxy had been in his arms. Like him, she was an early riser due to years of waking early to start baking for the deli. At the moment, she was still asleep, her body soft and pliant. He was spooned behind her and slowly pushed up on an elbow. It was Christmas Day and the weather had cooperated with a glorious snowy morning. It was barely light with the fluffy snowflakes drifting down brighter than the wispy gray sky.

He reached over to brush her tangled hair off her cheek. She opened her eyes and rolled into him. His body, which ran on high idle with barely leashed lust every moment she happened to be nearby, instantly tightened. She blinked her bright blue eyes and stretched. "We have to get up," she said, her voice husky with sleep.

"Right now?"

She nodded emphatically. "Uh huh. I have tons of baking and cooking to do before everyone gets here for Christmas dinner. Come on." She kicked the covers off and grabbed his hand. Seeing as he didn't want to be anywhere other than wherever she happened to be, he followed as she tugged him behind her into the shower.

Not much later, after he managed to steal a quick moment in the shower by stroking between her thighs to find her hot, wet and ready and sinking into her channel with one surge, he walked downstairs afterwards to find Roxy already whirling around the kitchen. She'd dressed in record time after they got out of the shower and dashed downstairs. He made his way to the coffee pot in the corner and poured a cup for himself. When he glanced her way and didn't see the usual coffee cup right beside her, he snagged another mug and filled it before carrying it over to her where she was rapidly rolling pastry dough for pies.

"Thought you might need some of this," he said as he held the coffee mug aloft before setting it on the stainless steel table nearby.

She flashed a smile and paused to set the rolling pin down before grabbing the coffee and taking a big swallow. "Oh thank you." She immediately picked up the rolling pin and got back to work.

"Okay, what can I do?" he asked.

It was barely seven in the morning. The sun was cresting the trees and the closest mountain ridge, casting a soft light through the tall windows running the length of the wall on one side of the deli kitchen. Today was friends and family only, so Max had planned to spend the morning helping Roxy with whatever she needed. She paused and brushed a loose lock of hair out of her eyes, leaving a smudge of flour behind on her cheek. She glanced to him and toward the back hall. "Would you mind pulling some stuff out of the refrigerator in the back? We have two hams and two turkeys. Diane prepped them yesterday, so they just need to go right in the oven."

"Got it." He took a quick gulp of coffee and left it behind as he strode down the hall to the massive refrigerator in the back.

By the time he returned with the first ham already in its cooking pan, Phoebe and Jake had arrived. Phoebe had thrown herself into helping Roxanne already, while Jake helped himself to coffee. The moment Jake saw Max, he came to his side. "Can I help?"

After Max set the ham on the counter by the massive wall oven, he gestured for Jake to follow. "We're on carrying duty," he said with a grin.

As they walked to the back, Jake spoke. "Heard from Hank the other day that DA's office finally filed charges against Wallace for manslaughter."

Max nodded. "Me too. He called late the other night and let me know." He paused, considering how he felt. He felt relieved and vindicated on his father's behalf, and mostly just damn glad the whole mess was over. Though his mother's choice not to tell him about her suspicions until years after the fact still rankled a bit, in a way, he realized it saved him from years of frustration and resentment. If Wallace hadn't gotten caught up in the shifter smuggling network, the police never would have had the leverage they did in the end. Wallace finally fessed up to leaving a wrench in the massive paper rollers in the hopes it would injure Max's father. The pressure that got him to cave was the authorities freezing what little assets he had left. Aside from Brad, Wallace's wife was living alone at the family's old property and had health concerns related to a heart attack she'd had after her oldest son died.

Brad had turned over all of the family's accounting information, which helped the authorities trace the money smuggled so many years ago. Hank had offered to give Max a chance to talk with Wallace himself, but he honestly didn't care to. He couldn't bring back his father, but he could rest easy knowing the truth had finally come out. He paused outside the refrigerator and glanced to Jake. "Thanks for your help with the investigation. Without the work you and Lily did, not so sure we'd have ever chased down who was responsible for the embezzling. That was the key to the rest."

Jake nodded. "Any time. I'm glad we finally know what happened. I know your parents aren't here to appreciate that fact, but I hope it helps a little."

"It helps a lot. I always knew I'd come back to Catamount, but it's nice not to have a cloud of questions anymore."

"Here's hoping I only have to do online forensics for boring stuff from now on," Jake offered with a wry grin.

Max swung the door to the walk-in refrigerator open. Over the next hour or so, he and Jake ended up being the unofficial runners of the morning. Long after they delivered the requested hams and turkeys to the kitchen, Max carried a platter of appetizers to place on the tables he and Jake had set up earlier.

The deli slowly filled with shifter families and other locals as the day wore on. Roxanne finally declared everything was just about ready and raced upstairs to change, leaving Phoebe and Shana to monitor the ovens for a few minutes. Max followed her and stepped into her bedroom upstairs a few minutes after she'd dashed off. Roxanne stood in front of her dresser, fiddling with her hair. His eyes caught hers in the reflection from the mirror above the dresser. With a roll of her eyes, she spun around. "I give up," she said, gesturing to her hair.

Honey gold waves tumbled around her shoulders. He stepped to her. "You look beautiful. Why are you worrying about your hair?" He reached up and sifted his fingers through the silky locks.

She lifted a shoulder in a shrug. "Because it's always half falling down, so I was trying to make some effort."

"It's perfect."

Standing before her on the first Christmas with her in fifteen years, his chest was tight with emotion. He threaded his hand into her hair and dipped his head for a quick kiss. "Just be you."

She glanced up, her eyes glistening. "You're here and it's Christmas." Her voice lilted at the end. She reached up and traced her fingertip along his jaw.

He let his head fall until his forehead rested against hers. "The part about being here wouldn't matter if it weren't for you."

She tilted her head up just enough to catch his lips in a kiss. In seconds, he was ready to take her right then and there. Footsteps pounded up the stairs. "Roxanne! One of the burners caught on fire!"

The moment was snapped, and Roxanne spun away. "What?!" she asked as she raced to the door where Joey stood.

Max gathered himself and jogged down the stairs behind Joey and Roxanne. Jake had doused the fire before they even arrived downstairs. After the small mishap, the gathering eased onward.

***

Roxanne leaned back in her chair and sighed. She

twirled her wineglass in her hand and took another sip before setting it down. Max's arm was thrown across her shoulders, and he was laughing at something Hank had said. She almost thought she should pinch herself. Less than two months ago, if someone had told her the one man who held her heart would be at her side at Christmas, she'd have laughed and tried to hide the tinge of bitterness underneath. Yet, here she was with him at her side. Against all odds, he'd knocked down the walls around her heart.

Hours later, after a leisurely clean up with the help of many of her dearest friends, she dried her hands on a towel and tossed it in the hamper in the corner of the kitchen. She heard footsteps and then Max pushed through the swinging door to the back hallway. He wore his winter jacket and held hers in one hand.

"Well, that's it. All the leftovers are covered and put away. It'll take us a week to get through it all, but it's done," he said.

She laughed softly. "I'll go through them tomorrow and parcel most of it to give away."

"Let's go then," Max said, holding his hand out.

"Where?"

He angled his head. "Just follow me."

"I hate surprises," she said as she approached and placed her hand in his.

He tossed her jacket over her shoulders as they made their way down the hallway. She followed his lead when he stepped into his boots. They walked outside. The air was sharp and icy. She paused to look at the sky. The snow had stopped falling a while ago, leaving a fluffy blanket over Catamount. The stars were bright against the inky sky. He gripped her hand firmly and gave a little tug.

"Come on."

Feeling silly, she tromped along behind him.

A Catamount Christmas

Catamount was quiet on this snowy Christmas night with not a car to be seen. He led the way to the town green. No one had shoveled the paths on the holiday, so they left a trail of footsteps in the snow behind them. Max stopped by the large Balsam fir in the center of the green, the holiday lights draped around it glittering in the darkness.

Her heart was so full, she could hardly bear it. He knelt in the snow and pulled out a small bag. Shaking the snow off, he lifted a small box out and handed it to her.

"I'd planned to give you this the Christmas after we moved away. I kept it all this time. Just like I meant back then, I wanted you to know I loved you and when you were ready, we'd get married. I hope it's not too soon to give you this. I'm not asking anything because I know…"

She cut him off when she flung herself at him, knocking them both over in the snow. "Yes!" she said when she brushed the snow out of her eyes and looked down at him.

"But…"

She struggled to sit up, propping her elbow on his chest. "Oh, now you're the one with all the 'buts.' I've had plenty of time."

His mouth quirked in a smile. She brushed the snow off his face and leaned down for a kiss. "I was ready to wait…just so you know," he whispered against her mouth.

She dropped a quick kiss on his lips, which were a warm contrast to the cold snow surrounding them.

"You haven't even looked at the ring," he said when she pulled back.

"Oh! Where'd it go?"

She clambered up with Max following. It took several minutes of looking in the snow to find the small box. Inside, she found a silver band dotted with sapphires. Amidst tears, laughter and shivers, they made their way back through the snowy night.

~The End~

Be sure to sign up for my newsletter! I promise - no spam! If you sign up, you'll get notices on new releases at discounted prices   and information on upcoming books. Click here to sign up: http://jhcroix.com/page4/

Please enjoy the following excerpt from **The Lion Within, Ghost Cat Shifters!**

Chapter 1

"Watch out!"

Sophia Ashworth glanced up at the sound of her
friend's voice to see a potted tulip tottering on the deck
railing just above her head. She had been looking down at
the slate walkway that wound around the deck at her friend
Vivian's house. Her eyes followed the bright red tulip as it
lurched from side to side before it toppled off the railing.
With a squeal, she dashed out of the way. She managed to
avoid getting conked on the head, but her shoulder was
covered in potting soil when she looked up again. The plant
pot sat cracked on the ground. She glanced up at Vivian to
find her covering her mouth in a weak attempt to keep from
laughing aloud.

Sophia rolled her eyes and brushed the soil off her shoulder before sifting her fingers through her hair. The tulip hung from the back of her hair. Carefully untangling it, she noticed its bulb had survived the fall. She held it aloft as she walked up the stairs to the deck.

"After all that, you'd better replant this poor flower." She handed the bedraggled tulip to Vivi and glanced around. "How the hell did that happen?"

Vivi had given up from holding back her laugh and simply pointed over at her cat, a black and white cat who was just barely past being a kitten.

Sophia strode over to the cat and swept him in her arms. "Jax, you are trouble!" She nuzzled her nose in his neck. His return purr was enough to vibrate through her entire body. Holding Jax in her arms, Sophia plopped down in a chair beside the small wooden table on her friend's deck.

Vivian Sheldon, Vivi to her friends and family, was Sophia's best friend. Lately, Sophia needed lots of Vivi time. Her brother Heath had been arrested two months ago when he was caught at a local drug dealer's house in the middle of buying heroin. At thirty-one, Heath was three years older than Sophia and had been her beloved older brother her entire life. After a car accident a year ago, he'd gotten hooked on painkillers. She thought he was finally kicking the habit only to discover he was so desperate for a fix, he'd tangled with the shifter smuggling network that had taken hold in Painter, Colorado. The only upside to the whole mess was he was now in treatment. Since his arrest was his first offense, he'd been given the chance to do treatment and community service. As long as he stayed clean for a year, all charges would be dropped at the end of the year.

Sophia stroked Jax's fur and glanced at Vivi.

"How's it going?"

Vivi was already busy replanting the tulip into another flowerpot. Her long black hair was pulled into a ponytail that swished from side to side when she glanced over her shoulder. "Same, same. Busy with work and arguing with Julianna's new first grade teacher. I'm telling you, before you have kids, you'd better think long and hard. If it were just me and worrying about what I did, it wouldn't be so bad. Try facing down the school if you're worried about something. Mrs. Dunn is a bitch," she said flatly.

Sophia nodded and commiserated with Vivi. As a single mother to Julianna, Vivi had plenty on her plate. Sophia was relieved to focus on something other than everything that had been weighting her down lately. Between Heath's car accident, his difficult recovery, and the most recent mess, she felt like she'd dominated just about every conversation she had with Vivi. She was trying to let go of what she couldn't control. Being a sounding board for Vivi's frustrations with Julianna's new teacher was a nice change. As she stood to leave a while later, Vivi caught her eyes. "Any news?"

Sophia's heart clenched as she shook her head. "Nope." With Heath away, she kept hoping for something to shine a ray of hope. She also kept hoping for something to give in the wall of silence around the police investigation into the shifter smuggling network. Before Heath had brushed up against it, she and just about every shifter who wasn't involved had been concerned about the network's existence. It was rattling nerves and raising fears of exposure for shifters in the absolute worst light. With centuries of secrecy protecting shifters, some shifters had forgotten how important it was. While she'd certainly been concerned about the network before, she was fired up and furious since Heath had tangled with it. She knew perfectly well he was responsible for his own actions, but the easy access to drugs had offered a path for Heath to stumble along. Heartsick over witnessing her once proud and strong brother fall so low after his car accident, she was bound and determined to make sure they exposed the shifters involved once and for all.

Vivi stepped to her side and tugged her into a swift hug. Sophia gave a small wave once she stepped off the bottom step and walked down Vivi's short driveway to the road. She lived only a few minutes away and walked by almost every day on her way to work.

Moments later, she walked down Main Street in Painter, Colorado, a picturesque little town high in the Rocky Mountains, tucked in a small valley. She pushed through the door into Mile High Grounds, the small coffee shop she owned. When she'd decided to start this little café a few years ago, she hoped it would succeed, but it had done far better than she hoped. She glanced around to see most of the tables full and a line that wound almost to the door. She couldn't help the tiny hum of pride. She lifted the counter opening and stepped behind it, grabbing an apron and tying it around her waist quickly.

"Hey Josie," Sophia said when she stepped to Josie's side by the espresso maker.

Josie was one of her two main employees. Sophia had a few others that filled in, but Josie and Tommy were her regulars. Josie moved lightning fast as she served one espresso and immediately prepped for the next. "Hey Boss. It's been crazy all morning."

"Looks like. Want me to take over this part for a bit here?"

Josie shook her head. "Nah. I'm good. Tommy could probably use a hand at the register," she offered with a nod toward the counter.

Without a word, Sophia stepped to his side and turned on the other register. The line started moving more quickly, and Tommy stepped back to help Josie crank out coffees and serve bakery items. Sophia was on autopilot, taking orders, ringing them up in the computer and processing payment. She bantered with customers and savored the busyness to keep her mind off of her brother and the constant worry her parents were carrying.

She glanced up at the next customer and her breath went out in a whoosh. The man standing at the counter instantly taught her the meaning of the phrase "took my breath away." A flush raced through her and her pulse quickened. The man was tall, dark and mouth-wateringly handsome. He had black hair on the longish side with dark curls edging the collar of his t-shirt. His navy blue eyes were bright against the contrast of his dark hair. His features were strong—sculpted cheekbones, a blade of a nose, and full sensual lips. His t-shirt was gloriously stretched tight across his muscles. She could actually count his six-pack of rock-hard abs.

She must have been silent a beat too long because the man arched a brow.

"Uh, what can I get for you?" she blurted out.

Wow. Pull it together. You sound like an idiot.

Sophia shook her head, trying to knock her obnoxious critic into silence. Oh-so-sexy man's mouth hooked on one side, his eyes glinting.

"Did I miss something?" he asked.

"Huh?"

"You shook your head."

She felt the heat race up her neck and face. *Maybe you should pay better attention to me sometimes. Shut up.* She sighed internally. She was having an entire conversation in her head while the sexiest man she'd ever laid eyes on stood there watching her and thinking she must be half crazy.

She met his eyes and forced smiled. "Oh, nothing. Coffee?"

His smile stretched from one corner of his mouth to the other. "That's what I came to find. What do you recommend?"

"It depends on what you like. Straight coffee? Or something more?"

"Something dark."

Dear God. The man had only said a few words and her heart was already racing, heat flooding her body.

"How about a double-shot Americano?"

"Perfect."

Sophia rang him up, while Josie got started on his coffee. Sophie couldn't help the curiosity. "Are you from around here?"

Oh-so-sexy shrugged. "Yes and no."

"What does that mean?"

"I was born here, but my family moved away when I was only three years old. I don't remember anything, but I always wanted to come back."

Her curiosity notched higher. Painter was a fairly small town. Born and raised here, Sophia knew almost everyone in town. If she didn't personally know them, she probably knew of them.

"Well, welcome back. I'm Sophia. There's a chance I might know your family. I've been here my whole life."

"Nice to meet you, Sophia. I'm Daniel, Daniel Hayes. My parents were David and Sarah Hayes." A blink of pain went through his eyes. "They both passed away in the last two years."

"Oh…I'm sorry." Her reply was automatic, but she

meant it. She was close to her family, so the idea of somebody losing theirs was painful.

Daniel nodded. "Thanks. It's life." He paused and took a breath. Josie passed over his coffee. Sophie took it from her and slid it across the counter to him.

He took a swallow of coffee and closed his eyes with a sigh. "Wow. Damn good coffee." When his blue eyes landed on her again, her belly fluttered. Her body appeared to have a mind of its own when it came to this man.

She couldn't say why, but his parents' names were vaguely familiar. She didn't want to pry, so she left it alone.

"How long are you visiting?" she asked, trying to keep focused.

"I'm moving here for the summer actually."

"Oh. You just decided to move here?"

His navy eyes held hers steadily. "Yeah, pretty much. My mother always talked about Painter and how much she missed it. After she died, I decided I wanted to come find out what she loved about this place."

Sophia nodded slowly. "Well, summer's a wonderful time to be here."

"That's what I heard." He started to say something else when another customer stepped to the counter. He lifted his coffee. "I'll get out of your hair, but I'll be back. I'll be needing more of this amazing coffee."

Sophia watched him turn and walk away, his stride long and loose. She forced her attention to the next customer. The day raced by. Late that evening, when the sun was falling down behind the mountains, she walked down Main Street, heading back toward home. Her eyes tracked the motion of her cowboy boots, the pointed tips alternating in her line of sight. She was weary from a busy day, but in any free moment, her mind wandered to worrying about her brother. The only relief she had came from wondering about Daniel today.

***

Daniel walked down the street, his eyes on the setting sun ahead. Painter was as beautiful as his mother had told him. The little town sat amidst the mountains, its streets winding along the hillsides. The view behind downtown was glorious at the moment. All that was left of the sun was a curved sliver above the ridge, bright orange with red and gold rays radiating into the sky behind it. Eyes on the sky, he suddenly collided with someone.

"Oomph!"

He looked down to find Sophia stumbling against him. Sophia was better known to his brain and body as the woman from the coffee shop who was so damn sexy he craved her as much as he craved coffee. Not even a single moment had passed since he'd met her for all of a few minutes and she'd been simmering in his mind all day. Her hands landed on his chest, and he didn't want her to move. One of his hands landed reflexively on her hip, while the other curled around her upper arm.

"I'm sorry! I wasn't paying attention." Her words came out rapidly.

"You and me both," Daniel replied with a wry smile. "I was looking at the sunset." He nodded behind her. She looked over her shoulder.

She turned back. "It's beautiful," she said softly.

Daniel nodded. He thought perhaps he should step back, but he couldn't. He felt the soft give of her hip under his palm. Her bright green eyes held his. A low charge hummed between them. He couldn't keep his eyes from flicking down. Her breasts pulled against the thin cotton of her black t-shirt. He forced his eyes up, only to have them land on her full mouth. He could see the flutter of her pulse in her neck, and he had to hold himself back from leaning over to drop his lips against the soft skin there. His arousal strained against his jeans, at which point he realized he was about to make a fool of himself. He shook his head and stepped back, his hands falling away.

He scrambled to recall what she'd said before his body had taken charge of his brain. *The sunset.* "It is," he said, his words coming out gruff.

Sophia's eyes held his, a green so deep he could lose himself in them. "I'll probably see you tomorrow if you're working again."

"Oh, okay."

As soon as the words left her mouth, Sophia rushed past him. He hadn't meant for that to be goodbye, but she seemed to have taken it as such. He turned and watched her walk away. Her dark hair hung straight down her back, swinging in tune with her walk. Her dark hair with her porcelain skin and bright green eyes was mesmerizing. When she'd looked up this morning, he'd wanted to reach across the counter and kiss her, right then and there.

Her hips swayed as she walked down the sidewalk. She wore purple leggings with black cowboy boots. Her leggings hugged her curvy hips and strong legs. Daniel watched her until she turned down a side street.

Available now!

The Lion Within, Ghost Cat Shifters

Go here to sign up for information on new releases: http://jhcroix.com/page4/

J.H. Croix

Thank you for reading A Catamount Christmas (Catamount Lion Shifters)! I hope you enjoyed the story. If so, you can help other readers find my books in a variety of ways.

1) Write a review!

2) Sign up for my newsletter, so you can receive information about upcoming new releases at http://jhcroix.com/page4/

3) Follow me on Twitter at https://twitter.com/JHCroix

4) Like my Facebook page at https://www.facebook.com/jhcroix

5) Like and follow my Amazon Author page at https://amazon.com/author/jhcroix

J.H. Croix

Catamount Lion Shifters

Protected Mate

Chosen Mate

Fated Mate

Destined Mate

A Catamount Christmas

Ghost Cat Shifters

The Lion Within

Lion Lost & Found

Diamond Creek Alaska Novels

When Love Comes

Follow Love

Love Unbroken

Love Untamed

Tumble Into Love

Last Frontier Lodge Novels

Christmas on the Last Frontier

Love at Last

Just This Once

Falling Fast

Stay With Me

A Catamount Christmas

When We Fall

Acknowledgments

A bow to my readers for cheering me every step of the way. The Catamount series was so much fun to write, and it warmed my heart that so many of you asked for Roxanne's story. As I wrote the series, she jumped off the page, so I was thrilled to make sure she got her own happy ending! Laura Kingsley keeps me on my toes with her editing. My covers are amazing entirely because of Clarise Tan at CT Cover Creations. Last, but never least, my hubby —couldn't do it without you!

Author Biography

Bestselling author J. H. Croix lives in a small town in the historical farmlands of Maine with her husband and two spoiled dogs. Croix writes sexy contemporary romance and steamy paranormal romance with strong independent women and rugged alpha men who aren't afraid to show some emotion. Her love for quirky small-towns and the characters that inhabit them shines through in her writing. Take a walk on the wild side of romance with her bestselling novels!

Printed in Great Britain
by Amazon